Taming A
Hurricane

by Paula A. John

Acknowledgements:

Comments and suggestions by Marie Alexander, Fred John, Polly Pattullo, Erik Schleef and Mikela Sonola led to changes to either the manuscript or the title. Thanks to all those who read or made comments as I went along, especially to Mike Martin, Jackie John and Sharon Johnson who read the entire manuscript or significant parts thereof.

All characters in this publication are fictitious, and any resemblance to real persons, living or dead, is purely coincidental.

Copyright © 2011 Paula A. John.
All rights reserved.
ISBN: 1452805512
ISBN-13: 9781452805511

For friends, family, God and country;
for Marie who encouraged me to write;
and for my daughters, Rhesa and Joda.

Chapter 1

My story is sketched in lost innocence and is written in the blood of my dead child. I had come to Dominica seeking revenge; instead, I found hopelessness and grief. I had come in strong but left broken. I had come with a plan but left with a jar of woes. I had come face-to-face with the devil himself: a devil by the name of Lennox King. But something had taken root in me that neither he nor suffering could take away; a seed so strong that I carry it to this day. This is my story:

My return to Dominica was furtive. I slunk in like a naughty child trying to bypass its parents. I told no one, and so, when I arrived at Melville Hall airport, there was no one to meet me. I had lost touch with everyone on the island, including my parents. Wanting to remain anonymous, I stepped out of the small aircraft into the warm, stagnant air of the late afternoon and hurried through customs, avoiding the gazes of those around me.

The view of Dominica from the air had been unexpectedly dramatic: dark, intense green, and row upon row of hills and jagged mountain peaks. Isolated settlements nestled grimly in narrow valleys, like bits of a sardine omelette splashed carelessly between the cushions on a sofa. It had all seemed very lonely and haunting, but, I suspect, that was the effect of all the greenery. *My Dominica*, I sighed, as I emerged out of the small terminal building into the undignified throng of waiting taxi drivers eager for a fare. I hadn't been back in many years, but I couldn't forget the land of my birth. Nor the monster who had used me as his practice mannequin. Now, I was back. Educated, sophisticated, and in control. Hell was about to break loose and this angel was about to do it. Or so I thought then. Time was to prove me very wrong.

I had booked a small hotel in the hills, some distance away from my native village, Salisbury—a small, former plantation house just outside of Cochrane. Cochrane itself was hidden away in one of the valleys, deep in the middle of the island, about sixteen miles from Salisbury. Access was via a long, narrow road, linking the west coast to the east, which wound progressively tightly as the altitude increased. The village was small and primitive, with a chapel and a patchy village school with meagre facilities. Most of the men hired themselves out on farms while the women either stayed home or found jobs in nearby Canefield or in the capital, Roseau. The Island Inn lay just on the outskirts, silent and solitary, but still warm and inviting.

I was a bit apprehensive about staying in such a remote location, mainly because I still remembered tropical nights with trepidation. Nights fell suddenly and were darker than most. A sort of thick, oppressive gloom which enveloped everyone like an unwelcomed blanket. Crickets chirped incessantly, and just about every firefly in the neighbourhood came out, blinking on and off in some sort of drunken ritual. Mosquitoes whined and snapped aggressively, eager for their evening meal. But the most disconcerting thing when I was a child was the haunting sound of dogs barking in the dead of night. The rumour in the village was that it was the sound of *lougawoo,* men who changed into dogs and attacked animals and people who dared venture out. I couldn't shake off these stories as I settled into my hotel bed, and I left the light in the bathroom on for good measure. I must have been tired, because all I sensed of my first night back in the tropics was its stuffy heat.

༺༻

"Mam, I have your coffee."
I woke with a start to a soft rap on the door and the reassuring cadence of the maid's voice.
"Come in," I mumbled, trying to sound more awake than I really was. In fact, I had been in a deep sleep when she called.
The rich aroma of Dominican coffee preceded her into the room. Nothing like the stuff bought off the supermarket shelves in the United Kingdom. Our coffee tasted of warm soil and wet mountains mists. It tasted of the stained hands which roasted and shelled the beans and ground them for our pleasure. It tasted of Dominica.
"What's your name?" I asked her as I sat up drowsily.
"Ruthina, Mam," she answered
Still sleepy, I chatted as she moved slowly across the room, pulling back the curtains to reveal already blinding sunlight. Ruthina had the very unusual colouring of a

shabine: cream-coloured skin with a riot of freckles all over her body that clashed with her bright red hair.

"Where are you from, Ruthina?" I asked.

"Salisbury, Mam," she answered.

I almost dropped my scalding cup. "Wha-what?"

She turned and looked at me curiously. "Salisbury, Mam," she repeated. A tad sharply, I thought automatically.

I just hadn't expected to find anyone from my native village working in such a remote place. I stopped talking to try to consider my options. This could be an excellent opportunity to update my database on my potential victim. On the other hand, the less of a trail I left, the better. Not that I was intending to murder anyone. My plan was better than that. But gossip spread like dust in a hurricane on the island, and I didn't want to be the talk of the village just yet. I came to a quick decision:

"How do you get to work, Ruthina?"

"I get a bus to Canefield Mam an then, di hotel have a bus to bring us up here."

"Do you know Teacher Lennox?"

"Teacher Lennox?" She echoed in surprise. "He living at Ti Tanse. He have a big house, boy."

"Oh, really? Is he married?"

"Yes, he married to dis white lady from America. I fink she teaching at his school. You know, one of those volunteers. Um…" She trailed off uncertainly.

"Oh you mean, a Peace Corps Volunteer?"

"Dat's it!" she piped triumphantly.

I smiled gleefully and let her go. More information than I had expected at this early stage. I went down to breakfast after a warm shower. It was hard to know what to wear on my first day back. As a "returnee,"

I was expected to dress up to show that I had "done well" abroad. On the other hand, the locals resented it if those returning home appeared too remote and standoffish. Then they were labelled "fresh." It was a difficult balance, but I settled on a pair of loose white trousers and a flowing, blue crinkled top. Little things mattered here. If you wore both white trousers and top, you risked being asked by a cheeky passerby if you were going to play cricket. So, safe in white and blue, I headed for the dining room, taking my notebook—my war book—with me.

The hotel was small and intimate, secluded behind bright, multicoloured bougainvillea bushes and tall bay trees. Only its green roof was visible from the road. I doubt there were more than eight rooms, but mine was tastefully furnished with a huge, four-poster mahogany bed and rattan furniture. Madras fabric, characteristic of the island, adorned the wide windows. It was all very Caribbean. The staff's uniforms were cleverly designed to incorporate the madras theme. The female staff, like Ruthina who had brought my coffee, wore madras pinafores of varying colours over white shift dresses, while the waiters and other male staff wore black trousers and white shirts with red sashes around their waist. This was the national attire for men and was favoured by many of the hotels across the island.

Breakfast was laid out on the open veranda overlooking the Caribbean Sea in the distance. Calm and blue at most times, dark and threatening during the hurricane season, it swept the western coast of the island. It was a beautiful day; a day which brought out the best of Dominica: calm, still weather and clear blue sky with a few friendly clouds grouping together in smoky puffs. The sea, almost silver in its brightness, lay shimmering beyond the green vegetation. A perfect day. Nothing to prepare me for the hurricane which was to sweep across my paradise.

The food laid out on the madras tablecloths was a serious Creole affair. There was *accra*—saltfish fritters—served with *bakes*, or fried dumplings as everyone called them in England. On another platter were sautéed *titiwi* small, translucent river-fish which looked like tadpoles. Chopped watercress and local hard-dough mastiff bread completed the selection, and then, my favourite hot beverage, cocoa tea—made from real cacao beans, roasted and ground and rolled into small cylindrical shapes, like fat sausages. The smell of the ginger and cinnamon used to spice the tea was overwhelmingly. I inhaled deeply and then sipped tentatively. Ah, very sweet. Just as I liked it.

I opened my war book as I sipped. Page seven. Lennox King. Age fifty-five or thereabouts. Teacher and child molester. Con artist and charity worker. Saint and sinner. *I'm coming to get you.* Wife. I updated my records. Children? Hope not. Didn't want too many bodies. Ti Tanse. That was a small, secluded bay not far from Salisbury. Just wild scrub with a treacherous path leading to the sea when I left. *Must have been developed into some housing estate or other*, I mused. I wrote carefully in capital letters on a loose sheet of paper:

DEAR MRS. KING, DID YOU KNOW THAT YOUR HUSBAND REGULARLY RAPED SCHOOL GIRLS? LOVE, A VICTIM.

I folded the note meticulously, put it in an envelope, and dropped it into my open bag.

"May I join you?"

Startled, I looked up. "Sure," I answered, looking into a pair of smiling eyes and a set of slightly crooked, yellowing teeth. It was the young man who had shared my taxi the night before. Fatigued, I had fallen asleep straight after getting in and hadn't caught his name. Neither had I noticed the little white collar which was now clearly visible around his neck. A priest? A visiting preacher? I was intrigued. And if any of the above, why speak to me? Shouldn't he be busy keeping holy?

"I'm Fenek," he said as he sat down. "Ian Fenek."

"Fenek?" That surname rang a bell. "Where are you from, Ian?"

"Malta. I'm from Malta."

I was speechless. A few years ago, I had spent a year or so working in Malta. Fancy meeting a Maltese here. A Maltese priest? But surely, he would be staying with one of the priests on the island, not here in a hotel? I couldn't contain my curiosity. Something else also niggled. That surname *Fenek* was significant. I was sure it meant something, but I couldn't put a finger on it.

"So what brings you to Dominica, Ian?" "Or is it Father Ian?" I added quickly. I thought for a moment that he looked a little uncomfortable.

But he laughed anyway. "Yes." He was an assistant priest. He looked a bit young though, for the honour. Surely he couldn't have been a priest long? Another embarrassed twitter. "Five years, my girl. I'm not as young as I look."

"So how old is old?" I had a rather bad habit of going for broke.

"How old do I look?"

Funny how *all* men respond in the same way when asked their age. You just never get a straight answer. I was bored of their game. This man looked no older than twenty-three, but I decided to have a go at deflating his ego.

"Hmm," I hummed thoughtfully. "That's a bit tricky. You could be any age, you see. But I can see the lines of wisdom around your eyes and mouth which say that you've led a hard life. I'll go for thirty-eight."

Father Fenek was not impressed. He looked instantly hurt, like a young puppy casually kicked aside by a previously doting owner. He swallowed painfully. "You mean I look *that* old?"

I laughed again, but more playfully, this time. "No, I was just joking; I guess you're about twenty-five at the most."

His relief was almost tangible. "Oh, you got me there," he chuckled, wiping his brow in mock relief. But he still didn't give me an answer and I decided to leave it. I wanted to know other, more interesting things, like what he was doing in Dominica. But my brain swung into motion all on its own, and I exclaimed rather triumphantly, "*Fenek*, that means 'rabbit' in Maltese, doesn't it?"

Ian was genuinely surprised at my knowledge of his native language. "You speak Maltese? But how?"

"I don't really speak it," I admitted. "I just know a few words. I lived in Malta for a while."

"Wow! That really is impressive. I wasn't expecting to find anyone here who'd been to Malta. Apart from my friend," he added quickly. And then more hesitantly, he said, "You wouldn't happen to know a Patsy Serrant, would you?"

He said *Serrant* like an English-speaking person would, pronouncing each letter, including the final *t*. But in Dominica, we said it like the French would: *sayrã* with a nasal at the end.

"Patsy Serrant?"—I said it our way—"No, but I've been abroad for a long time. Why, did you meet her in Malta?"

Ian smiled but didn't answer. I guess such matters were delicate. Maybe I could reassure him and get him to confide in me. I sensed a love story there. Why else would he come all this way asking for a stranger? He obviously didn't have her address, or he wouldn't have asked me.

"Is she your friend, Ian?" I asked again, very gently. "Are you looking for this girl? Don't worry, I don't live here, I won't tell anyone if you tell me." I smiled reassuringly like a loving aunt. He was pouring some juice and didn't answer.

Then, he carefully buttered some toast as if his work would somehow be inspected. Or maybe he was just buying time. Then suddenly he said, "I'm in love with her."

I tell you, I honestly dropped the bit of bread I was about to put in my mouth. "You, you are? But aren't you a priest?" I blurted. I was genuinely confused. He probably was as well, for that matter.

"I'm still in training," he acknowledged, after an imperceptible pause. "But I've got to take my final vows later this year. I need to be sure, you see. That's why I came."

And here I was, thinking I had problems. Now *that* was a problem. I encouraged Ian with a few more questions, and he seemed happy to share his story. To be honest, I don't think he had a choice. There was no one to talk to but me. So, on my first day back in Dominica, I became mother confessor to a priest, of all people.

I listened intently as Ian told me about his childhood, growing up in an orphanage in his native Malta. It was run by the church in Sliema. "Yes, I know the home in Silema," I assured him. I had lived nearby and worked in a hotel on Sir Adrian Dingli Street. As a matter of fact, the view of the bay across to St. Julian was the reason I had decided to return to Malta for an extended stay after my first holiday there. It was breathtaking with the roofs of brightly-coloured sun huts peeping through a rich array of trees and shrubs overlooking the sea. I thought, then, that the whole of Malta was as beautiful and captivating as that bay. There had been no visible sign of the xenophobic current which was slowing seeping through their society.

Ian told an interesting tale of his conversion and subsequent call to the priesthood: one day, he had been sitting waiting to go to his first confession. Being last in the queue, he watched as each of his friends went in sullen with repressed anger and emerged relieved and happy. He was intrigued by the transformation and had resolved to find out more about the church that claimed to have the power to forgive sin. He slowly became obsessed with the rituals and mystery of the altar. The smell of incense became a forbidden aphrodisiac. As he served as an altar boy, he imagined that its heady bouquet was the perfume of a mother he had never known; the sweeping skirts of the priest's vestments, her swishing robes. The bread placed on his tongue healed his broken soul. Having forgotten his mother's mammary offerings, Ian fed each Sunday from the priest's extended hand, knowing instinctively that somehow, his beloved 'mama' had found a way to offer him her love. He was immensely grateful and, when he reached adulthood, decided to become a priest. He would continue the cycle and feed the healing bread to others. He was completing a placement with the University Chaplaincy when he met Patsy—a free-spirited young lawyer doing a postgraduate year at the Law Institute, right next to the university.

"She must have been really beautiful then, to get you to fall for her," I commented, when he paused. Ian pulled out a crumpled photograph and showed me shyly, as if not trusting me to approve of his choice. I reached out and took the photo, eager to see the girl who had stolen his heart. They were sitting on a low wall, he with his arm draped comfortably across her shoulder and she resting hers casually on his knee. Ian wore an open-necked dungaree shirt, showing a very tanned throat. A slim gold chain glinted around his neck, but there was no priestly collar in sight. The girl appeared friendly and happy, her broad smile revealing a wide gap in her teeth. But she was no beauty: her sparkling eyes bulged out of her face, and her cheeks stood rigidly at attention as she held her smile. Like a happy frog. She appeared quite flat-chested, but her hips sprawled loosely over the bench, taking up twice as much room as Ian's.

Ian waited expectantly as I inspected the photo. "Nice," I offered, handing the photo back. "But how did you two come to fall in love?" I was genuinely intrigued. The girl just didn't seem like his type. She was too...ordinary. Ian, even with his dog collar, was sleek and virile.

He looked away and I wondered if he were embarrassed. But he went on to explain how he and Patsy had finally fallen in love. He had taken her sightseeing one afternoon, and she had slipped and ended up in his arms. Seizing his opportunity, he had pulled her close and kept her close. He noticed little things about her then: the smell of her hair, the warmth of her breath, the thud of her beating heart. He was afraid to let her out of his arms in case she never returned. When she lifted her head to meet his gaze, he thought he should apologise and opened his mouth to do so. But she mistook his parted lips for an invitation and pressed her warm ones against his. Ian explained that he was lost after that. He started forgoing his duties to meet with Patsy. Sometimes she would attend service at the church in Gzira and then stroll to the marina on Manoel Island, where they would conveniently *bump* into each other. He would then offer her a lift home, and they would spend hours talking in his parked car. Things came to a head when Patsy asked for a good-bye kiss the evening before leaving for Dominica.

"I lost my soul then," Ian mumbled.

I barely caught the words. His head was buried in his hands and he rubbed his temples back and forth, as if trying to caress her memory.

I looked away. Ian's story made me uncomfortable. I wish I had minded my business and not invited his disclosure. He sighed, and I turned to him again, wondering what sort of lover he would be. He really was attractive in an uncommon sort of way. I mean, one would have to get used to his features. His skin was burnt brown, but even so, it couldn't obscure the wide expanse of his extra-broad jaw. Droopy eyelids framed dark, slanting eyes, and his hair curled in a shapeless haircut. He gave off a raw, restless energy, like a frustrated animal. It was unsettling.

He looked up and met my inquisitive gaze boldly. I moved my chair back instinctively. Ian was dangerous. I'm sure he was. Too sexually charged for a priest. I looked around suddenly and realized that the other guests had gone. The waiters had started clearing the tables, but I had been oblivious to the clinking of the crockery. I had been lost in Ian's fairy tale. My war book still lay opened at my elbow.

Ian, too, must have thought he had said more than he intended, for the shutters came down over his face. He cleared his throat and stood. Short, I noticed and instantly lost interest. I didn't relish towering over my mate.

"Why don't you check with the staff at reception?" I asked as he looked at his watch. "This is a small island; someone's bound to have heard of your friend."

He nodded briefly and strode away. Hands in pockets and head tipped upwards, he appeared a proud, confident man. But I wasn't fooled. Proud, confident men fell for proud, confident women. Patsy didn't fit the mould. But I had no more time to give to Ian. I, too, was on a mission—I had a rapist to find. I headed for my room to make contact.

The maid must have been in to tidy up because my bedcovers were pulled back neatly and my shoes were paired and left in a straight row at the foot of my bed. I felt an instant irritation. I didn't like strangers arranging my things. There was a telephone directory beneath the phone next to the bed, and I searched carefully, relieved to find the name I was looking for. I wouldn't have liked to go through the receptionist.

"Hello?"

"Hello. Is that Lennox?"

"Yes, who's dat?"

"Merc—umm, Agnes."

"Agnes? Who's Agnes?"

"Agnes Vincent," I said calmly.

Silence. Heavy breathing at the other end.

"Agnes," he whispered.

"Yes, can I see you?" I asked, getting straight to the point.

"Agnes, I'm married. Yeah OK. Hold on."

The scraping noise sounded like he was changing phones. Then in a conspiratorial whisper, he said, "OK, Agnes; when can I see you?"

"You tell me."

"Tonight, OK. Actually, why don't you come round tonight. We're having some friends over."

"Are you sure?" I was incredulous.

"Yes, no problem; I'll come and get you."

We arranged a time for the evening, and I went back to the reception to enquire about getting to town. I needed some clothes, something bright and tropical. And maybe I could help Ian find his girlfriend. Do an evil deed and cancel it with a good one. The bus left every hour, I was told. With another half hour to go, I flopped into one of the oversized chairs on the veranda. I looked round for Ian, eager to continue talking about his experience and his homeland.

In many ways, Malta was my second home, a surrogate island which stood in for Dominica when I was desperate for the sight and smell of the sea. But there was little else in common. It was perhaps more like Barbados: a small, inhabited rock set adrift in the middle of the sea. While Dominica was a verdant paradise, Malta was a stark, white, rocky oasis. The endless prehistoric limestone was broken only by huddles of white buildings and patches of short, intermittent vegetation forming a broken green carpet. It was so different to Dominica that I found it entrancing at first. Very Mediterranean. Initially, I had loved the men's dark good looks, but with time, I saw more of their faults than their charm. I wondered if Ian would like Dominica. We were definitely less stuck on tradition than the Maltese were, with rum drinking the new national pastime of our country.

I spied Ian sitting in a corner in animated conversation with one of the other guests. A slim, blonde-haired girl from Eastern Europe, I guessed. Maybe Russia? She didn't speak much English from what I could overhear. I wondered how she came to be in Dominica. Our world was certainly becoming smaller and smaller. I watched slyly above the top of the newspaper I pretended to read. Ian, for all his inexperience, seemed to be doing rather well for himself. His whole body was curved in her direction, a subtle signal that she had all of his attention. He laughed often, throwing back his head and baring his teeth. It was an open invitation to admire his masculinity. The girl herself looked a little timid. She couldn't have been more than eighteen. I wondered if she were there with her family.

I looked impatiently at my watch just as the horn of the minibus trumpeted noisily at the front. We all got up on cue and headed for the door. I went in first and made a beeline for the backseat. There was plenty of room, and I wanted to give Ian the opportunity to sit next to me if he wished. He didn't, and I remained alone at the back. But it afforded me a good vantage point to keep an eye on the action. I was having second thoughts about our Maltese visitor. I wondered if he were a flirt. Then I started pondering on why he insisted on wearing his priest's collar, since he was in Dominica on affairs of the heart. Surely, he would want to be a little more discreet? I decided to keep a sharp eye on Mr. Fenek to see what his game was. He barely glanced in my direction and sat next to the long-legged beauty, leaning over and whispering into her ear as the bus rolled on. But I did see him show her Patsy's picture. Maybe he was innocent after all. I would wait and see.

Soon though, I had other matters to deal with: matters of safety, of life and death; our driver's unspoken quest for the afterlife on a gleaming Saturday morning. We clung on desperately as he did his death dance, whizzing past other vehicles along blind bends and shouting obscenities at the poor pedestrians unfortunate enough to be on the road. It was frightening. After a particularly scary flight past a 3-tonne truck, I decided to speak up.

"Man, why you driving so fast? *Mwen pa vini aisi —la mor ou sav,*" I said, letting him know that I hadn't come here to die.

Presumably shocked by the flow of Creole from my hitherto European tones, the driver, still at top speed and just approaching a bend, whipped his head round for a penetrating look. "Ay-ay, lady you talking *Kweyol?* I take you for some British lady, man."

"Well, I'm British, but I'm a Dominican too. Slow down this damn bus. You want to kill everybody or what?"

"OK, Mam. Sorry," he said sheepishly.

By then, Ian was silent and grim-faced, hanging on determinedly and staring stoically into the distance. I wondered if he were on a silent phone call to heaven. Or maybe he was thinking of his girlfriend and hadn't noticed that only fate or God stood between him and death. But then, coming from Malta, he was probably used to flamboyant driving. The fact is that the only other place I had felt so distinctly unsafe on the roads was in Malta. Road safety didn't appear to rank highly on the Maltese driver's list of priorities. Whereas Dominicans chased the thrill of speed, foolishly liking the narrow winding roads to flat, specially designed racetracks, the Maltese flagrantly flouted every traffic rule obstructing their progress: turning the wrong way into one-way streets, failing to stop for pedestrians - even children. I spent most of my time there dodging death on the roads.

Well, it was good while it lasted. Malta was in the past. I was back in my homeland, ready to face the challenge I had set myself. Lennox had been placed on the back burner, but not forgotten. Hostilities had been suspended but not curtailed. I was ready for revenge: "Lennox, be afraid; be very afraid," I whispered, feeling invincible. But, in a small unacknowledged corner of my heart, I was bleeding slowly to death.

"Okay, we here!" our driver announced. He had just landed his 'airbus' in the capital.

Chapter 2

Roseau was hot, as usual. For some reason, it always seemed to be the hottest spot on the island. I think it got its name from the reeds growing along the river where it had sprung up as a settlement all those years ago. Marcus, the bus driver, had stopped right outside the market, believing it a good place for tourists to start discovering the town. I didn't think he was wrong. On Saturday mornings, virtually the whole island converged on the market. Farmers came from all over to sell their produce. It was also a convenient place to sample local specialities and to meet people. I was going after some black pudding, myself. Made from a mixture of pig's blood, bread, and spices, it was not for the fainthearted. My other favourite was what the locals called *fashine*—cow's hide that was roasted to facilitate the removal of short hairs, then cut into pieces and marinated in lime, chives, peppers and onions. It was then cooked to a sticky consistency.

I had a warm feeling inside. All this food was part of me, part of my identity. When I thought of Dominica during my self-imposed exile, I remembered not only the people I had left behind, but also the food we ate, the games we played, and the languages we spoke. I also thought about our festivals and music. I wondered what Ian would make of Dominica. Would he find his girl? Would he be welcomed by her family? Would he get used to the strange food and quirks of the people? Would he fall in love with the natural beauty, the rivers, the waterfalls, the sulphur springs, and the salty sea? Would he be ignored as a stranger or invited into their homes? I think it would mostly depend on how he engaged with the locals. If he worked his dark charm, he could have them eating out of his hands—especially the ladies.

That reminded me, where was my dashing stranger? Ian was nowhere to be seen. I looked around, loathe to abandon him on his first day. I spotted him eventually at the other end of the market. He wasn't alone though. He was guiding the blonde gently through the crowd with a well-placed arm on her elbow. I decided to forget about Ian. I wasn't sure what his plans were, and I didn't have the energy to find out. I was back home now, back on my beautiful Dominica. I needed to get to know her again. Reacquaint myself with her sights and smells, with all the things which made her special. I searched people's faces as they went about from stall to stall, enquiring, negotiating, complaining. But I recognised no one. Some people looked familiar, and at times, I made eye contact eagerly, hoping for a flash of recognition, some acknowledgement. I received barely a smile or a courteous nod. These people were at home going about their daily lives. I was just another number in the crowd.

I bought a young *jelly* coconut, just as an excuse to stand still. A group of men from the Carib Territory were selling them off the back of a pickup truck. Jelly coconuts were just young coconuts picked before turning hard and dry. Harvested at the right time, both the sterile water and soft jellylike flesh inside could be intensely sweet. With time, the flesh hardens to become the white kernel which can be grated and mixed with water to get coconut milk. Although satisfying, my nut wasn't as sweet as I remembered. I suspect that their popularity as a tourist commodity meant they were harvested much too early. A bit disappointing for the other people from abroad who had gathered around the truck, trying a much-hyped product. They all "oohed" and "aahed" appreciatively, but a wry twist of the mouth here and there betrayed their true sentiments. I was restless, strangely burdened. I was searching for I knew not what. Slowly, I strolled away from the noisy market.

Roseau was a small, compact town trapped between the sea, a river, and high, vine-covered cliffs leading up to the small suburb of Morne Bruce. From there, one had spectacular views of the town beneath. Most of the older buildings in Roseau dated from colonial times, and the ornate wrought-iron balconies and wooden louvre window frames still spoke of historical Creole connections. These window frames were known as *jalousies*, which is French for *jealousy*, and I like to think that's because one could peek discreetly at the competition strolling down the street without fear of being observed. It was hard to get lost in Roseau. Not only was it minute in size, but the streets were laid out in a fairly modern design of parallel lines. Plus, because of the river, there was only one way in or out of the town to the north. A southerly road led to the tip of the island and another one further inland to the Valley area where you would find the Trafalgar Falls and Freshwater Lake.

I had always thought that Dominica was shaped like a penguin standing still, in profile. Up north, around the protruding nose section was the town of Portsmouth. Salisbury, my native village, was on the western coast along the fat belly, and Roseau lay to the south where the land tapered off to form the legs. Soufriere, a small fishing village, rested peacefully at its feet.

Walking around Roseau, I could see real signs of change. For a start, there were many more businesses, most of which were housed on the ground floor of the two-storey buildings which characterized the town. Everything looked clean, and gaily painted benches, which doubled as advertising stands for local companies, were dotted around. Some parts looked completely revamped. The dirty, smelly slum area called the Gutter was no more to be seen. In its place stood a few modest blocks of flats and a proud, new government office building. Expensive cars and new minibuses flashed by. But people were a lot heavier than I remembered. Not that slim was ever really in, but the swaying hips and backsides appeared broader to me. I looked in fascination at the antics of one particular buttock, which seemed to drop steeply from a straight but broad back. It did a full rotation on the left leg, but on the right stride, it seemed to stop halfway, do a fluttery dance, then pause as if unsure of its next move, before completing another full rotation on the left stride. And on it went, until its owner disappeared. A little later, an older woman carrying a cardboard box filled with local produce on her head struggled past. She was most likely heading for the market, her face twisted with the discomfort of her burden. Slow trickles of sweat wound down her face close to her hairline, then branched off into rivulets underneath her chin. I could hear her exhaling deeply, every expired breath ending in a soft groan. She seemed to carry singly, the combined burden of the children of Adam. I wondered if she had any children and if, like me, they had moved on to greener pastures, leaving their ageing parent to fend for herself. No one looked at me. Everyone was intent on their purpose, but in general, people looked happy as they milled about, laughing and calling out to each other. Except me. I felt strangely alone, like an outsider spying on the locals. Like a visitor in my native land.

As usual, when I felt pensive, my thoughts strayed to Lennox. I kept hoping I'd bump into him and I caught myself looking fully into every male face, searching for his features. They must have thought me brazen because a few looked boldly back, sometimes turning around to keep my captured gaze. I didn't mind. I was used to the public courtship rites between the sexes. Men openly showed their interest here in Dominica. If you didn't mind their attention, you'd slow down and have a chat. If you did, then you'd suck your teeth noisily and flounce off, giving them a dirty look as you walked by. I was so used to being stopped in the streets that when I first went to Europe, I had wondered what was wrong with me. Why weren't the men eyeing me and letting me know that I was desirable? I quickly learnt that that just wasn't the way. But now, once again, I was basking in the sunshine of free love.

But I couldn't stop thinking of Lennox. I wondered what he looked like now. I hoped he was bald and stooped with bloodshot eyes, a huge beer belly, and hairy ears. I hoped he had lost his job and roamed day and night in the village begging for bread and for somewhere to lay his head. I hoped he was childless and that women refused his advances, preferring to lie with a beast than with him. Stuff it! Ruthina had said that he was married to an American woman. What kind of woman was she, then, marrying an ox like Lennox? Which reminded me, I needed to post the letter I had written to her. I was about to upset her world. Enlighten her about her charming prince.

I still needed to find a clothes shop. I wanted something cool and colourful, something to complement my ebony looks. I hadn't seen Lennox in more than twenty years and wanted to look my best. I was coming in strong and confident, ready to take on my adversary. But inside, I was empty, hollowed out. I had carved a deep hole in my emotions and filled it slowly with bitterness, cynicism, and indifference. While I had kept a book of revenge planning different delights for the man who had stolen my soul, I had virtually blocked the event itself from memory. I couldn't bear to remember. Mostly though, I felt guilty about having made myself available to be abused. And why hadn't I told my parents? My dad would most certainly have slaughtered Lennox and I would have lived happily ever after. Instead, I had allowed that horrible day to grow in awfulness and take possession of my life, my innermost being. I hated Lennox King. I hated all men. Awful creatures, they were.

"Mercury! Mercury!"

I came out of my reverie at the sound of my name. Okay, before you start getting confused. My name is Mercury Agnes Vincent. People from my village called me Agnes, but the girls I went to school with in Roseau called me Mercury. Sometimes, even I got confused.

"Mercury!"

It was my friend Marcia. My very dear friend, Marcia. She had taught me so much about myself and about life; how not to take things too seriously, and how to cope with the things which had happened to me as a child. She was always positive, always encouraging. She had no time for self-pity: "You're in charge now," she'd say to me again and again. "It's up to you to make something of your life." Finally, I believed her and took control of my future.

"Mercury, girl, when you come?"

"Last night. I arrived last night. Marcia, how are you?"

Marcia looked good. Smooth, dark complexion with slightly jutting teeth. She walked with a light skip and hop, like a flighty bird. She had her daughters Rhya and Evageline with her. Like me, she had never married, but unlike single me, she lived with her girls' dad. She was blooming all over. Third baby, maybe? I didn't ask. After all those years, I still remembered that Marcia was very secretive and didn't give up information about herself easily. I chose to remain on safe ground.

"So, how are you, Marcia? What are you up to? Tell me all, tell me all," I begged excitedly.

She had given up her job as a preschool teacher to start her own sewing business in her village. Apparently she was quite successful at it, and had been chosen to design and make the evening gown for the last Carnival queen who came from there. I could well believe it. Marcia was resplendent in a brown-and-gold African print ensemble, her long dread locks pulled up in a crown at the top of her head. She looked like a serene princess. I told her that I was shopping for an interesting outfit.

"Check out Boutique Domnik," she said. "They have some nice clothes. Well, you'll have to come and see me," she said. "I'll make you something nice. Wow, but Mercury, you doh change at all. Look at you; look at that flat stomach. You haven't got any children?"

I laughed. "No, no children. And no man either."

"Come to prayer meeting with me and I'll get you one," she promised and laughed.

I left her soon after, thinking about our conversation. At forty, I'd never been pregnant. Mostly because I'd spent most of my youth trying not to be. Now, I wasn't sure that I could cope with a baby. As for a man, well, I could think of other things I'd rather acquire. It was good to be free. Prayer meeting? Not for me either. God hadn't looked after me when I needed him as a child, and I didn't need him now. I could fend for myself, thank you. Plus I didn't like emotional encounters. Some of the prayer meetings I'd seen were just too extreme. Knowing Marcia, she probably was a high priestess or something.

Tall and proud, feeling good about myself, I made my way to Boutique Domnik, not knowing that before long, I'd be on my knees crying out to God.

༺༻

Evening came and I waited for Lennox to pick me up from the hotel. I would have welcomed someone to talk to, but Ian was nowhere to be seen. The other guests, a young Canadian couple on their honeymoon and a Korean businessman, were all occupied with their dinner, and I didn't interrupt. I didn't see Ian's blonde friend either. I wondered if they were together. I had learnt from one of the staff that her dad was actually the manager of the hotel. They were from Poland, and she was studying at the American offshore medical school in Portsmouth, in the north of the island. Apparently, she stayed at the hotel at weekends and during the holidays.

Her dad was a widower, his wife having died suddenly at breakfast one morning. The police had investigated, but the verdict was a simple heart attack. Both husband and daughter were said to be heartbroken. No wonder she looked so sad, I thought. Ania was an only child. I wonder how her dad would feel about Ian hovering around his treasure. You never know, he might actually welcome the idea of a son-in-law. *A son of the cloth.* I laughed bitterly.

I'm not sure why I was in such a bad mood. Maybe I was miffed that Ian no longer sought my company. Plus, I had foregone dinner and was hungry. Lennox had promised to feed me. The beast was late. Typical. I sat impatiently on the veranda sipping lime squash and fuming. I always tried to be on time and hated being kept waiting. I was a little nervous, though. I hadn't seen Lennox since leaving Dominica twenty years ago, and before talking to the maid in the morning, I had had no real news of him. I didn't even have a mental image of him anymore; just a deep, aching sore in my heart for my stolen innocence. My essence hadn't been mine to give. It had been brutally extracted from its inner sanctuary and I had lain sullied and bruised, while Lennox writhed, grunted and then shuddered in some sort of demonic ecstasy.

The only thing I never forgot about that moment was his face. But I can't talk about that now. Too painful. I got up abruptly and started pacing the veranda. As if on cue, a pickup truck pulled into the yard. It turned out to be a driver sent by Lennox. Lennox couldn't come himself apparently, being busy getting ready for the evening ahead. I greeted the driver—Melvin, he was called—but hardly made any conversation on the way to the village. The ride was uneventful, and since it was dusk, there wasn't much to see. The western coast of Dominica is fairly nondescript anyway. Shrubs and rock, with a few villages dotted at intervals along the main road leading from the south to the north of the island. Dominica was known as the land of rivers and in reality, most of the villages had sprung up along river courses. Only, the majority had now dried up and only flowed sporadically with heavy rainfall.

We passed the hamlet where my mum lived, but I said nothing, and we carried on to Salisbury. Salisbury itself is set on a hill, overlooking a bay which sits at its feet like a watery offspring. The Bay, as the seafront is known, was home to the cemetery, an old school building, and an old police station. When I was a child, it was also an important docking point for the banana boats making weekly visits to transport bananas to England. The local fishermen also set off from there in their canoes for their daily catch. Then, the Bay was full of life and an integral part of the village. The local church also stood right there at the entrance. Ti Tanse, where Lennox lived, was a little farther on, past the road leading into the main community. But there was no need to go through the village to get to Lennox's, and we carried on.

There was a small guesthouse right there on the main road—which, by the way, the locals called the Highway—run by one of my aunts who had returned permanently from England. Hilda's Hotel, the sign announced. There were chickens scratching idly at the front, but no other sign of life. Aunty Hilda was my great aunt, and I had visited her regularly while she lived in Britain. But after retiring from nursing, she decided to head back home. She had never married and was childless. Attractive woman, though, and quite well spoken. I had asked her once why she had never married, and she had snapped, "Men are all jerks. Put them in a room with a bowl of milk and eventually, they'll put their privates in it." Hmm. I guessed that she had had her heart broken by such a man. At least she'd lived to tell the tale. Some women were not that fortunate.

It was now well and truly dark, but soon after, we turned off the main road on to a stony track. The stones were just wide enough to support the wheels on each side of the vehicle, but I could see the outline of the grass growing in the middle. It was uncomfortably bumpy, and I hung on to the strap swinging over my door.

"Doh worry, man; we soon arrive," my driver assured me.

I smiled slightly, a bit embarrassed that I had let my discomfort show.

We drove past a couple of lighted houses along the track, and then up ahead, previously obscured by some acacia trees, stood a solitary house. It was hard to tell exactly, but I decided that it could only be Lennox's, since there were no other houses in sight. I could see a few vehicles parked outside, and music was blaring. People were tripping in and out, laughing and talking excitedly.

"I turned to the driver in surprise. "Oh, is it a party?"

"Nah, man, just some members come over."

"Members?" I was confused.

"Yo! Hang on, I coming," he called out to someone in the yard.

Then we pulled up and I tumbled out of the truck, quickly rearranging my clothes as I looked up into his smiling eyes. Lennox's, that is. My breath literally stopped. Gosh! The guy was breathtaking. Soft brown eyes, even teeth. Warm complexion like unrefined brown sugar. A short, sharp haircut and neatly trimmed beard. Both hair and beard were speckled with white. Sexy. He was intensely sexy. I felt the power flowing through him and was lost.

"Agnes," he said, in a warm, slow voice.

I tried smiling but couldn't speak.

"How are you, baby?"

His voice was like honey trickling over a sore throat. For a few seconds, I closed my eyes and just let it wash over me. This strong, comforting man, could he be my rapist? I paused briefly, trying to let my senses guide me. I prided myself on reading people's vibes. If this man were evil, I would sense it within seconds of meeting him. My whole spirit would reject him. I stood still for a few seconds... Nothing. Just the warm aura of a strong man.

I opened my eyes slowly and looked fully into his. "Hi, Lennox. How are you?"

He pulled me close and wrapped me in a hug. He smelled of citronella. Something stirred sharply against my thigh. I smiled triumphantly to myself. *OK, you're human. I've got you!*

Lennox led me inside, still holding on to my hand. His friends smiled and greeted me as we went past.

"Come meet Susan," Lennox said.

"Susan?"

"My wife."

She rose, smiling as we entered. She was heavily pregnant. A tiny, dark-haired girl. Well, young woman. Twenty-five, I guessed. She extended her hand just as Lennox was saying, "Sweetheart, this is my friend, Agnes."

"Agnes, how nice to meet you."

Susan had a makeshift Salisbury accent, betraying straightaway a desire to embrace all that was her husband's. I liked her. She looked like a simple girl. Slightly crossed-eye. No airs or graces. I relaxed and started looking around me.

"Pastor, we ready to eat, you know. You going to pray?"

I turned sharply and saw one of the ladies addressing Lennox. Pastor? *Pastor? Please tell me this was a joke!*

Lennox didn't meet my gaze but looked directly at his guest. "Sure, Lizzie; get everybody. I'll pray."

"Heavenly Father, we thank you for this gathering." The same warm tones of a beautiful man. "Thank you for each other and for our friend, Agnes. We pray that she might know you, even as we do. Bless this food and the hands that prepared it. Amen."

I couldn't accept this. I searched frantically for some opening. I needed some air. A door. I stumbled through onto the veranda. Oh my God, I thought, please tell me this isn't true. I think I could have accepted anything but this. Lennox had raped me when I was only ten years old. He had been about twenty-five, then, and had taught at the village school. I know for a fact that my friends Victoria and Karen had suffered the same fate. God knows who else he had abused over the years. Now he was this perfect man with a perfect house and a perfect wife. And a bloody church to go with it!

"Be still, Agnes; Be still," I said to myself. I had become my own counsellor over the years. My own friend, my own keeper. I loved myself because no one else had loved me. *Always a winner, Agnes, always a winner.* I hadn't noticed that I had started calling myself Agnes again. In Europe, I was Mercury: tough as nails, tall, and proud. Agnes was my other self, the girl who had been too weak to defend herself, too weak to report it. The girl who had almost spoilt my life. I didn't trust her.

"Agnes, there you are."

It was Susan. She laid a hand on my arm. I turned to her and smiled, looking at her huge tummy. "How far gone are you?"

"Almost there now," she said and sighed.

"So Lennox is a pastor?" I couldn't help it. I needed to know more.

"Yes." She laughed. "Didn't you know? We have a church up in the village. Lennox is such a godly man. I am so blessed to have a husband like him."

Yeah right, like I hadn't felt his manhood stirring against my leg. "So how long have you been married?" I enquired instead.

She giggled. "It was love at first sight. We met at a training day in town. You know, at the Teacher's Training College."

Her voice trailed off as someone came through the door. I couldn't face anyone else and blindly opened the wrought-iron gate at the end of the veranda and dashed out into the dark evening. I breathed in deeply and tried to take in my surroundings. I hadn't realized that the house was so near the cliff. The soil was too poor to grow much, so Susan had a few plants in pots dotted around the yard. A few coconut palms and four or five Flamboyant trees separated the property from the cliff's edge. Flamboyant trees were my favourite. They spread out like large canopies, providing easy shade in school playgrounds and village playing fields. More and more people were planting them on their properties, I would find. Night had fallen, so it was hard to see any of the intricate red flowers or crescent-shaped pods the trees produced.

I walked around looking for a way down the cliff to the bay beneath. I needed to be alone. I found some steps round the side of the house and started down. I thought I heard my name, but I didn't stop. Steps had been carefully hewn out of the sheer rock. Some of them were covered in moss, so I doubt Lennox had done that. Ti Tanse was a popular bay with villagers during the crab season. The crabs came out with the rains and crawled over the country-side risking death as they crossed the roads. But the intrepid villagers liked to go down to the sea to catch their own fresh. It was quite an adventure going crab hunting.

The men lit up *bouzayes*, homemade flaming lamps. They poured kerosene into empty bottles and forced a cloth through the opening, leaving a portion to act as a wick. The parties wound their way eerily along the cliff, finally disappearing over the edge—like stars shutting down for the night.

The stars were just coming up now, and I was grateful for their light as I inched down. I shouldn't really have been doing this. There was no one to help me if I fell and broke a leg or something. Plus, I was scared of the dark. I could hear the waves lapping gently as they broke on the shore. It was comforting in a strange sort of way. The sea was alive, and I needed life. Someone or something that I could trust. Two more steps, thank God. Blessed sand. Yes, peace.

I'm not usually such a reckless person. I hadn't done too badly for myself, in fact. I left Dominica as a twenty-year-old and headed for England, armed with a few pounds and an aunt's address. One of my cousins had trained as a nurse, and I quickly followed in her footsteps. I liked nursing but never managed to shake off the overwhelming sense of responsibility attached to the job. What if I made a mistake and killed someone? I left the profession as soon as I could. I took a language degree after that and taught for a while at a local college. But I was a restless soul. I was a prisoner of my past. Every relationship ended in dust. I had tried young men and old, black and white, educated and simple. I hated them all. They were all horrible. Maybe I was the horrible one. Maybe it was time to see this thing through, time to face the demon at the top of the cliff. Time to lay Lennox to rest and let the flower in me blossom.

At forty, I knew that I couldn't continue like this. I was tired of running away. Now, I would try anything. I wanted to be whole again.

I found a smooth rock and sat facing the sea. For once, I wasn't afraid of the night. I needed to hide in its shadow. The darkness was warm and gentle. The stars, unblinking in the sky, seemed to keep guard. Maybe I should confront him in public, right there in front of his members. I had posted that letter to his wife and was planning to take out an ad in the local newspaper: Is there a rapist near you? it would ask. I was planning to upset everything he had worked for, get him fired from his job. But I hadn't counted on him leading a church. How could such an evil man become a pastor and talk in the name of God? Even having the cheek to ask God to touch me. Brute beast!

"Agnes! Agnes! Oh, there you are."

It was Lennox, just negotiating the bottom step. He was alone and carried a torch. I just looked up dumbly. I couldn't speak. He sat next to me and put a comforting arm around my shoulder. He was so strong, so safe.

"Lennox"—I looked at him beseechingly—"can you just say you're sorry, and I'll forget about it?"

"Say sorry?" He looked confused. "For what?"

I recoiled somewhat. I hadn't expected that either. "For raping me!" I said sharply.

"Raping you?" He moved away, stung. "What? Is that what you have been telling people? That I raped you?"

His eyes sparkled with anger, and he didn't touch me anymore. His face was clouding over, and I suddenly felt cold. But I was not about to back down. I had waited all my life to confront this man.

"Are you going to deny it?" I asked incredulously, fixing him with my now-hardened gaze.

"You bitch, you come to make trouble? Well, I never raped you. How's that?"

This really had taken me by surprise. I never counted on Lennox denying events. Not in private, to me, at any rate. I decided to use the last bow in my quiver.

"Well, what about Vicky and Karen?" I asked, still hard and brave.

"Victoria and Karen are members of my church," he spat. "Would they be sitting in my church if I had raped them?" He looked triumphant.

That was the last blow. There was nothing further I could say.

"Agnes," he said to me, calmly, "I like you, but I won't let you destroy all that I've worked for. You mess with me and you'll regret it!"

His gaze was piercing and direct. The look of a confident man. I stood still, saying nothing; just gazing at the black sea, wishing it would swallow me.

His gaze softened as he reached for my arm. "Come on. I'll take you home."

Chapter 3

I had moved out of the hotel and in with my mum. She had rung imperiously one morning and summoned my presence. "*Ti fi, ou vlai di mwen ou Domnik eveh ou pa vini weh mwen?*" She was angry that I'd been in Dominica and hadn't gone to see her. Anyway, she ordered me to pack my bags and make my way home. So I did. I bumped into Ian just as I was leaving the hotel. He too was waiting with packed bags. I was intrigued and asked if he were leaving, if he had made contact with his friend, Patsy. He nodded and just said soberly. "I'm a dad."

"A dad?" I was incredulous. "How do you mean?"

Ian bowed his head, understanding my confusion. He hadn't told me all that day. He and Patsy had come together that afternoon. He hadn't known that she was pregnant when she left. She never contacted him, and he probably would never have found out about his child if he hadn't come to Dominica.

"So, are you going to stay with her? Is that why you're leaving?"

Ian stood abruptly and started pacing. "How much time do you have, Mercury? Can I talk to you?"

"Sure," I answered. "Come, let's find somewhere private." I led Ian out into the yard, to a bench under one of the large nutmeg trees. I didn't want to miss my brother who was on his way to collect me, so we sat just off the main path. "So, what's up then, Ian?"

"Mercury, I'm not really who I said I was. I'm not a priest at all."

I waited.

"I'm actually a lecturer at the Law Institute, and Patsy was my student. I'm sorry I lied to you, but I had to have a cover for my visit. It was just easier to pretend to be a priest. I really was brought up in a home and all that, but I was never a priest."

I must say that I was relieved. I have always trusted my instincts, and I am rarely wrong. A trainee priest searching for his love just wouldn't advertise the fact in the way Ian had. "So what will you do then, Ian, now that there's a child?"

"Well, here's the big problem. I'm already married. Patsy doesn't know that and might expect me to do the right thing. But I've got a wife in Malta. She's gone on an extended visit to her relatives in Australia, so this was the perfect opportunity for me to come here looking for Patsy."

"Ian, this is really serious!" I exclaimed. Then I fell silent, pondering.

"Things haven't been great at home," Ian continued. "My wife can't have any children, and we bicker and fight all the time. But we can't get divorced. Maltese law doesn't recognise divorce."

I had forgotten that. Now Ian *really* had a problem.

"Well, maybe it's time to pray, Ian. I really don't know what to say to you."

Tears trickled down Ian's cheeks as he spoke. I hadn't thought about how this might affect him. To be honest, I usually had very little sympathy for men. As far as I was concerned, they deserved everything they got, and it was okay for a few to pay for the sins of many. But with Ian knowing that he had a child, a child he'd always wanted but wasn't free to embrace, that must be hard. So I had the grace to feel some pity. Plus, it wasn't up to me to judge his ethics. I was no saint and could easily have been in a similar situation if things had turned out differently for me.

"It looks like you are moving out, Ian. Where are you heading?"

"Patsy's coming to get me in a little while. You know, she's doing okay. She's got her own practice and her own home. I'll move in with them for a while."

Something occurred to me, suddenly: "By the way, Ian, how did you find her, eventually?"

He laughed. "I found her within half an hour of being at the market. I just showed her picture to a few people. One of the stall owners was her aunt!"

He laughed again, relieved no doubt that things had worked out so easily. But the real problems would lie ahead as he strove to unravel his complicated love triangle. I gave him my mother's phone number just as my brother turned into the yard. A quick peck on the cheek and we parted company. Strangers with a bond of two islands.

I spent the next few days hibernating, getting to know my family again. My older brother lived at my mum's with his girlfriend and their two children. My mum still ruled with an iron fist, but she was slowing down. She was now in her late sixties. I remembered her as a young, vibrant woman raising a family of five under difficult circumstances. My father had died in an accident just before I was born, and my mum remarried when I was about three. It was a difficult marriage with lots of beatings and abuse, but the end came when my mum caught my stepdad in bed with a young girl from the village. She had rammed a broomstick up his naked backside and had kicked and clawed at the girl who ran out of the house unto the road. She was naked except for a bra dangling off one arm. She begged piteously for her clothes and tried to hide her nakedness with her cupped hands. My mum stood guard with her broomstick, shouting abusively and laughing like a crazed woman. She defied the girl to come back in to fetch her clothes, saying "*Vini, si ou sai fam,*" Creole for, "Come, if you're a woman," which meant, "Come if you dare."

Eventually, I couldn't stand the embarrassment any longer and ran back into the house to collect the girls' clothes. I could hear my stepdad groaning in the bathroom, no doubt from the soreness of his rear. I rushed out again, past my mum who was still waving her arms and swearing in Creole. She reached out and tried to grab my skirt as I went past, not wanting the humiliation of her adversary to end. But I eluded her and flung the clothes over the fence to the girl. By then, a small crowd had gathered, laughing and jeering. My mum continued her ranting, but after the girl left, she turned to the crowd, filling them in on the details of her story. I crawled away silently, heading for the haven of the bushes at the back of our house. That was, undoubtedly, the most embarrassing day of my life. My stepdad left for the United States soon after, and I never saw him again. Then, my mum, too, moved out of Salisbury to Mero, where she still lived. Funny though, all these years later and they never divorced.

But, for me, being part of a family again was difficult. My mum told me when to get up and when to go to bed, when to go out and when to come home again. Which is why, on that particular Sunday, I was on my way to church with her. The invitation had been brutal: "What kind of pagan are you, sitting in my house and not going to church? Come on, girl; put on your clothes. I leaving in ten minutes." So I did.

My mum still went to church in Salisbury, although there was a perfectly decent chapel in Mero. After church, she did the rounds of friends and family. She had lost her mother a few years earlier and kept an eye on various ageing relatives.

"Oh, aren't we going there?" I asked, as we drove past the church. The Catholic church was the very first building along the main road as one approached Salisbury, close to the bay which I mentioned earlier. My great-grandfather had built it with a team of masons before I was born. The whole village seemed to congregate there on a Sunday morning. The cemetery lay opposite, impractically, within a coconut grove.

"I'm born again now," my mum answered shortly to my query, and my brother sped on to our mystery destination.

"Christ's Temple" was emblazoned in bright colours on the outside of the building, each letter in a different colour. We were late, and the discordant sound of drums greeted us. An equally unmusical choir was in full chorus: "*Then sings my soul, my saviour God to thee; how great thou art, how great thou art; then sings my soul...*"

We entered the doors and my heart almost stopped in shock. There on stage, resplendent in priestly robes, was Lennox. I stumbled, and my mum turned impatiently and hauled me in. *Oh please God, not this, not here.* I cried silently.

Lennox was seated in a throne-like chair on stage while his choir sang around him. His eyes were shut in apparent contemplation, and he hadn't seen us come in. I noticed Susan at the front, flanked by two "sisters" in madras headdress. Lennox himself wore a flowing white gown like a priest but had a large madras sash around his neck and a black turban around his head. That was unusual. Men didn't wear turbans in Dominica. Part of his priestly image, I guessed. The choir came to the end of their torturous routine, and someone introduced "our beautiful pastor."

The transformation was magical. Lennox leapt to his feet, and the congregation followed, waving in excitement and anticipation. "Faithful one, so unchanging, ageless one, you are my rock of peace, holy one, I depend on you, I cry out to you, again and again, I cry out to you, again and again."

Lennox's voice rang out in pathos, strong and clear. He cried out his love song to his God, and his members swayed, carried along on his wave of love. The atmosphere was electric. It was charged with something that

I couldn't put my finger on. Something had happened when Lennox started singing, but I didn't know what it was. Women were crying and men hunched over, blunt fingers covering their eyes. My mum was in full swing, calling out words of praise in a loud voice.

I stood and watched, and, as if drawn by my gaze, Lennox lifted his head and looked straight at me. I didn't discern any surprise. He shut his eyes again and carried on with song after song.

"Thank you, everybody. Sit down. Our God is good. The Lord has sent me to heal the brokenhearted, to proclaim liberty to sinners. To turn the hearts of fathers to their children and children to their fathers. I am the Lord's messenger. The glory of God is in this church," he continued. "We are God's chosen people."

Please tell me that I am not hearing this, I thought. *This could not be real!*

Lennox carried on with his preaching and then started prophesying. "There is a woman here with an issue of blood. You have bled continuously for twenty-five years. Please stand up. God is ready to heal you."

I looked around, interested. Silence. Then slowly, a little old woman towards the back of the church got to her feet. The church erupted in rapturous applause. Lennox was ecstatic. "Come here, Ma," he called. "Come, let me pray for you."

The old lady made it down to the front with the help of two of the ushers.

"Our sister has been bewitched for the last twenty-five years," Lennox continued. "But the day of her deliverance is at hand. *Be gone!*" he shouted and plastered his hand on her head.

She seemed to crumble, and fell into the waiting arms of the ushers. They laid her down in peaceful rest.

Lennox took a deep breath and turned back to the congregation. "There is a woman here," he said, "you were raped as a child. Since then, you have joined the synagogue of Satan. God is going to use me to release you."

Outraged, I stood up, making my way down through the row of seats to head for the door. Lennox was prancing triumphantly around on stage.

"Clap for Jesus, clap for Jesus," he repeated over and over.

I got to the end of the row, and the waiting usher grabbed my hand, leading me to the front. I protested feebly. *Oh no, they thought I had stood up in agreement,* I groaned inwardly. But I was at the front, and it was too late. I was on stage with Pastor Lennox, and he was prophesying over me.

"Lady, you were ten years old when you were raped by a man. No one knows this but you and your God. Not even your mother. Since then, you have gone from man to man, rejected and unwanted. No man wants you. No man will marry you. You are doomed to a life of sorrow unless you turn to Christ."

I am ashamed to say that I burst into tears. There he was, my rapist, prophesying over me, condemning me to a life of bondage, unless I joined him in his farce. Is that how he got Vicky and Karen to join his church, I wondered. He was stretching out his hand over me, in prayer.

"Father, into your hands, I commend her spirit."

An overwhelming force hit me right in the pit of my stomach. My feet buckled, and I ended up in a heap on the floor. I was conscious. I could hear what was going on, but I couldn't move and couldn't interact with my surroundings. I made many attempts in my spirit to get up, but I couldn't move a muscle. In the end, I gave in to the most amazingly beautiful feeling of peace.

Chapter 4

My mum's response to the revelations was characteristic. She upbraided me for keeping "my dirty secret" and ordered me to move in with "Pastor Lennox and Sister Susan" for "further deliverance."

"Never!" I said, and stood my ground. For about two weeks. But my mum wasn't a woman to be trifled with, and, of course, I gave in eventually. *"Mwen pa vlai piess diab a kaye mwen"* she said every time our paths crossed. She didn't want a devil in her house, but she seemed bent on sending me to the devil's house! I changed my mind, however, when my brother brought home a pleading note from Susan. She was sorry she'd not had a chance to speak to me that day at church, would I come and keep her company for a few days? I was sure my mum had engineered it, but it didn't matter any more. I was tired of fighting. So, like a lamb, I went to the devil's lair. It changed my life forever.

༄

Susan was nearing the end of her pregnancy and was very tired. She spent most of her days lounging on the veranda. She slept a lot, but I felt she looked a little troubled when awake. Lennox was away most of the time, going to the different villages, holding healing and deliverance clinics. I think he was relieved that Susan had company, so, he stayed out late. I hardly saw him and we didn't speak again of the events of that Sunday. Instead, I helped Susan prepare her baby's *layette*. The women in her church had given generously, sewing and crocheting tiny clothes for the new baby. Some days, they brought nutritious soups for the pregnant mother. *Callalou* was an all-time favourite, made with young, tightly curled dasheen leaves—a local equivalent to spinach. Dasheen is a tuber, like yams, grown in swampy patches of land.

Susan bloomed under all the love and care but the tiny lines around her eyes and mouth remained. She came to me one morning.

"Did you send this?" she asked, pulling my letter out of her pocket. I had forgotten about that letter.

"Yes," I responded, looking at her steadily. There was no point in denying it.

"Is it true?"

"Yes," I said simply.

"I'm really sorry." She was almost in tears.

"Thank you. It was a long time ago. Don't worry about it."

"I need to show you something," she said, unbuttoning her blouse.

I looked at her in surprise. She had a determined look on her face, but said nothing. Her fingers were fat and clumsy. Her breasts were also swollen in pregnancy, and slowly, she peeled open her top. Bit by bit, she revealed her bruises. I gasped as she showed me the bite marks on her breasts and the purple wheals on her back. Some had faded, but there were fresh ones replacing the older ones in a sort of crisscrossed jumble. I felt sick.

"Did he do this to you?"

"Yes."

"Susan, why don't you leave him?"

"I can't," she admitted. She looked up beseechingly. "I love him, Agnes."

"But what would your mum say, Susan? You, out here in the Caribbean being beaten up by some strange man?"

"I'm an orphan, Agnes. I've got no one on earth except for Lennox."

I understood her plight. But how could she love a man who used her as a punching bag? That, I couldn't understand. But never having been in that situation, I couldn't judge Susan. Plus, she didn't need a judge; she needed love and support. So, I helped her as best as I could.

But something strange happened one day. Susan was out on the porch fanning herself and sifting tiredly through the bags of baby's clothes at her feet. She exclaimed impatiently as she realized that she had forgotten something inside the house; a blanket she had brought over from the States. Her own baby blanket which she kept permanently at the bottom of her suitcase. It went wherever she did. She made to get up, but I pressed her arm. "Don't worry, Susan; just tell me where it is and I'll get it for you."

"Oh thank you, Agnes, thank you."

The blanket was in a brown suitcase beneath the bed in her bedroom. I had been in there, many times with

Susan. It was just a plain room with a large wooden bed and two wardrobes in a corner. So I went straight to the bed and reached underneath. Nothing. I reached blindly a few more times, but made contact only with air. So I got down on all fours and looked under the bed. Indeed, there was a brown suitcase tucked away in a far corner at the back. There was no way Susan could have reached it in her condition. I had to half crawl beneath the bed, but I got it in the end. It was a striped, battered thing with two old-fashioned sliding locks. Actually, it looked just like the old suitcases we called a *grip*. It was quite dusty, in fact, like it hadn't been opened in ages. I opened it carelessly, expecting, of course, to find Susan's blanket. Instead, there was a stack of papers, all tied with a bit of twine. And a book. I picked it up slowly, looking at the title: *Ancient Book of Magical Arts*. Not what I expected. It was a big, impressive-looking book, like a bible; of a rich, navy colour. The letters were embossed in a now-fading gold. But the most curious thing was the cross on the front: it was pointed at the bottom like a dagger and the top end was curved, like a crook. But still, it looked like a cross. Intrigued, I opened the book, my heart beating erratically. Why would Susan have a book on magical arts, I wondered. Unless it belonged to Lennox! Surely, he should be getting his power from above?

I scanned the table of contents, conscious that Susan would soon notice my absence.

1. Magical Arts of Ancient Egypt
2. Gog and Magog
3. Secrets of Babel

4. A Day in the Life of the Witch of Endor
5. What Daniel Couldn't See
6. Setting up Your Fellowship

I flicked to the latter, sure that this was where Lennox had got his ideas for his church. *"The minds of the people are the gateway to their soul,* it said. *Capture a mind and you have a slave for life. Serve not a slave, but use it for your pleasure. No part of a slave is sacred from its master. Initiate a slave in its infancy and benefit from a life of power. The flower of youth is the candle to your soul."*

I was so engrossed in reading that Susan was at the door before I heard her. I slammed the book shut and stuffed it back into the case, giving it a mighty shove back to the corner where I had found it. When Susan entered, I was still kneeling on the floor and looked up with a confused expression. "Susan, I'm sorry. I can't seem to find your suitcase. What colour did you say it was?"

"Uh, Agnes, I'm sorry. I just remembered that it's not under the bed, after all. Look, it's here with the other boxes, next to the window."

"Gosh, no wonder I couldn't find it." I made an excuse about needing the toilet and left. I was shaken by what I had read. I wondered how long Lennox had had that book in his possession. Had it fed his devious appetite through the years? Had I been one of his "youthful conquests"? I would never know the answer, for something happened which changed our lives irrevocably.

༄

It was incredibly hot. One baking day followed another. We were too hot to move. There was hardly any point in drying oneself after a shower. Susan waddled around like a stuffed duck, impatient for the end of her pregnancy. She was becoming more and more withdrawn, not responding even to her beloved ladies who came to help. I offered a few times to return home, sensing that she could probably do without the presence of a complete stranger. But each time she urged me to stay. Lennox seemed to be strategically choosing to stay away from home—from me, perhaps, but also from his responsibilities. Susan's burgeoning stomach was a constant reminder that his errant days would soon be over, and he fought that possibility with dogged absence. Then one day, without warning, the weather changed. The sky crowded with restless, roaming clouds. The sea started churning nervously. We couldn't put a finger on it, but something was wrong. Lennox himself came home unexpectedly. "There's a hurricane on the way," he said. "We've got to get ready."

Susan hauled herself up from her chair and headed for the kitchen. I followed silently. She opened the cupboards, removing all the dry goods and stuffing them into old sugar bags. She looked like a robot programmed to go through set moves. I began filling with water, all the bottles, jars, and buckets I could find. Susan seemed too bemused to speak; she just opened and stuffed, opened and stuffed. I, too, was silent. I thought about life and about how unexpectedly things changed. Life took us to places and brought us events that we couldn't foresee. I mean, there was no way I would have come to Dominica if I had known that a hurricane was likely. My parents had told us stories about the hurricanes they had lived through as children, and I did not want to be a part of it. Strangely enough, my thoughts went straight to Ian. I wondered if he were still in Dominica. A hurricane would not be a welcomed adventure. Lennox bellowed my name from outside, breaking into my thoughts—he needed my help boarding up the windows and reinforcing the corrugated roof. Still preoccupied, I joined him, but barely looked at him. He barked his orders—"Pass me that board. More nails. Lower."—and I responded like a puppet. My limbs went through the motions, but my mind was already shutting down, seeking the safety of hibernation from the stress.

I was very nervous. Somehow, I knew this was serious. As soon as we finished our preparations, I headed for the guest room and packed my things. I collected a few items from the bathroom as well. If there was going to be a hurricane, I would go home. I hovered as Lennox turned on the radio. There was only one local radio station and it served as the official voice for anything happening on the island—deaths, news, public notices, addresses from the prime minister. It was the only way to keep abreast of events. There were detailed instructions about how to prepare for the hurricane and how to keep safe. Every village had a designated hurricane shelter, and the announcer reeled of the location for each village. We already knew that the primary school was the designated shelter for Salisbury. Lennox said that we would stay at home.

"I need to go home to my mum," I protested hotly.

"Your mother will understand," he retorted. "I need you to stay with Susan. I have to visit my members."

By then, it was late afternoon. I couldn't realistically leave Susan alone, so I stayed. We finished our preparations and went to bed early. There was nothing more to be done. Personally, I was hoping we would just sleep through the hurricane. Maybe by the time we awoke in the morning, it would be all over. Lennox must have returned late that night because he was already awake and finishing a few jobs in the yard when I got out of bed. Susan was pottering in the kitchen. The wind started picking up by mid morning. It started as a stiff breeze, increased to a driving gale and finally became a relentless storm. At first, excited, Susan and I peered through the slits in the shutters, like children, curious of the strength of the mighty beast. There were windows in every room, affording views of the village in the distance or the sea beneath. But when the winds began to roar, we grew silent, conscious that the fiend was growing into a monster that could not be tamed. Even Lennox looked pensive. But I was glad he was home. He made me feel safe. For a brief moment, I wished things were different between us – he a dashing prince and I, his beloved princess. Sweet dreams, Agnes.

The house was of a typical construction: bathroom and kitchen in cement blocks and the rest of the house in wood. When the storm increased, we moved to the kitchen area thinking it better protected. Plus, the toilet was nearer for Susan, who needed it frequently. When the roof started peeling off, we scuttled like frightened rats into one of the back rooms. The hurricane raged well into the morning, numbing our spirits and filling us with despair. Our home was under siege. The wind seemed to howl with contempt as it battled against the boards and nails used to reinforce the windows. It was intent on breaking in. And slowly it did. Every window conquered brought our enemy closer, until, defeated, we retreated into a corner and huddled together for comfort. I don't know when I started praying. It seemed to come from a distance. I cried to God for mercy, asking him to stop the wind. By then, the radio station had stopped broadcasting. Our neighbours had opted for the hurricane shelter in the village. We were alone, certain of our impending death but not knowing at exactly what hour it would come.

When nature called, we answered in a bucket, in full view of each other. We felt no shame. Our foe had reduced us to animals. But Lennox and I grew increasingly worried about Susan. She seemed drawn to the lone window, pressing her nose against the moist glass and looking through the shutters. She was losing her fear of the beast and, instead, watched with fascination as objects flew past her post. She began a faltering commentary: "There goes a tyre" or "The mango tree is down."

"I need to get out," she said at one point, without warning.

"You what?" Lennox roared. "Are you off your head?"

Susan turned to him, a strange, pleading look on her face: "I need to get out, Lennox."

Lennox must have sensed her need, for he pulled her close, whispering reassuringly. Soon, miraculously, the winds abated, leaving a dead, unexpected calm. We whooped and scurried out of hiding, navigating through the wreck which was the rest of the house. Our previous refuge lay open like a sightseeing bus, letting in the elements.

Outside was a wilderness. Trees uprooted, electricity posts lying across the track leading to the house. We gazed in awe at the damage to our beautiful surroundings. Even the sea looked beaten and sullen. Susan picked up her ruined plants, that is, the ones she could find, and shed silent tears. There was a sudden gust, and Lennox came running towards us.

"It's not over yet," he called urgently. "It was only a lull. Come on; get back in!"

Scared, I bolted in straightaway, heading directly for our refuge. Lennox came in just as the wind returned with a screaming howl, tearing through the front door, searching for new conquests. The battle had recommenced. Lennox and I looked at each other: "Where's Susan?" We both shouted simultaneously, looking around feverishly.

Lennox ran to the solitary window, calling out at the top of his voice as he did.

"Oh my God," he whispered as he got there.

"Agnes," he said piteously, turning towards me. "Susan…"

His voice trailed feebly as I rushed to join him at the window. My heart stopped. Susan was naked, kneeling, arms outstretched at the base of the last-standing coconut tree in the yard, her face lit in ecstasy. The tree swayed as if intoxicated, its roots streaming out of the ground like dreadlocks behind a motorbike rider.

"*Susan!*"

Screaming, Lennox made a move towards the door. But he caught the same movement I did, and he stopped, entranced. Susan, arms wide, welcomed the coconut tree as it fell over her naked, pregnant body, her arms closing over its trunk in a wet, macabre embrace. Her baby squelched out noisily, joining her in a final bloody encounter.

The wind raged on.

Chapter 5

Dominica was completely devastated by Hurricane Drake, which had stood over it and raged blindly for a record twelve hours. Not a single leaf was left on the trees. They all stood on the hillsides naked and bare, pleading silently to be covered anew in their rich green foliage. Entire villages were destroyed by mudslides and rivers which had broken their banks. Bridges and roads collapsed, cutting off coastal villages and remote settlements. All essential services were disrupted. Dominica was in a state of upheaval.

At Lennox's, when the winds had finally abated, we crawled out of hiding like insects out of hidden nests, the fallen night shielding us from much of the horror around. We prayed over Susan and her child and covered them with a wet sheet. There was nothing more we could do until we had notified the police. Lennox and I went back into the only room left standing and lit a hurricane lamp. We tidied up as best as we could and settled down to an empty, deathly still night. Sobs wracked my body and Lennox held me tight, stroking my hair and then my face. We hadn't washed all day, and both of us smelled earthy and strong. But it was a reassuring smell. We were alive. Lennox and I came together that night. I forgave him for the past, for the memories which had held me captive over the years. I forgave him for abusing and enslaving me. I forgave the last thirty years and offered myself in an aching sacrifice.

But the next morning, with Susan's crushed body still waiting in the yard, I couldn't look at Lennox. I left quietly and headed to my godmother's in the village, leaving my belongings behind.

It was painful to see my beloved village lying wrecked and flattened. Rubble and litter were strewn all around. Salisbury had become a large, uncoordinated rubbish heap. People walked aimlessly, exchanging stories about where and how they had survived the hurricane. Two elderly people had died, and overall, thirty people had lost their lives on the island.

In the days to come, we ate what we could—fallen fruit and washed-up vegetables. Later, villagers ventured farther up into the hills, bringing down fallen bananas and plantains and distributing them amongst their neighbours. Also, most people still had a supply of dry and canned goods. Central government was nonoperational, but every village had an elected representative who slowly got teachers, nurses, and other professionals to co-ordinate recovery locally. The village school was still being used as a shelter for the homeless when I left Dominica, many months later.

I thought again about Ian Fenek and wondered if he had managed to leave before the hurricane. I don't know why I kept thinking of him. I think his story touched me more than I realized. I knew so many people stuck in unhappy relationships. Most of them never had the courage to free themselves. Most were trapped in the until-death-do-us-part doldrums.

I didn't believe that God meant people to live out their lives depressed and unfulfilled, with a partner who was either abusive or indifferent. Surely, "for better or for worse" meant facing the unexpected or unforeseen situations which presented themselves during the course of a relationship? I didn't think it was a call to sit like a fool while your partner treated you like dirt by having affairs, not contributing to the home, getting drunk or high on drugs, not being interested in you or your relationship. I was pleased that Ian had decided to pursue love, but cheating on his wife and getting another woman pregnant were hard to defend as a code of conduct. But thankfully, that wasn't my problem. Surviving after the devastation of the hurricane was. Years of progress had been washed away in half an awful day.

Surely enough, after the hurricane, it was "all change"—back to basics. We went back to cooking on open fires. Wood was plentiful, and most households reverted instinctively to the skills which had been overtaken by modern living. Very slowly, houses were patched and roofs re-covered. Relief supplies started coming in from abroad—canned corned beef hash, beans, dried milk, rice, and flour. Relief centres were set up, and we queued for family rations. Quite a colourful vocabulary sprang up post hurricane: clothes sent from abroad were known either as *bro-go-do'w*, a sort of onomatopoeic imitation of the destructive noise of the hurricane, or *ma-feh-sa*, Creole for "I didn't make this." You got a bit more ration if you knew or were related to any of the people distributing the supplies. Looting also became widespread, and people literally carried fridges, wardrobes, and beds on their backs—need and greed imbuing them with Herculean strength.

But, in general, all was peaceful. My godmother, Ivy, was in her early eighties. A small, thin woman, she had the characteristic freckles and fair complexion of the ladies in her family. She wore her two long plaits wrapped around her head or tucked under her madras scarf. Like the other islands of the Caribbean, Dominica reflected its colonial past in the shades and textures of its people—dark or fair, curly or straight, freckled or plain. Recessive genes showed up unexpectedly, prompting unsuspecting men to doubt the paternity of their offspring: "How could a black man like me make this red-skin child?"

Ma Ivy was a "sassy" woman. She flounced rather than walked, tossing her hair insolently at the many people she had managed to "vex with" in the village. Village *maipwi* bouts were notorious: women clashed in head-on mud-slinging sessions with former friends or neighbours. Everyone gathered around, cheering and leering, eager for the secrets which would be revealed by now-embittered friends: "*Sati salop*"—you whore—"*ou pwon mawi mama'w*"—you took your mother's husband.

It really was hilarious listening to these women as they destroyed each other's reputation. Men, of course, didn't "take out maipwi." They just fought each other.

In her heyday, Ma Ivy managed to ostracize most of Upper Salisbury where she lived, and now that she was old and frail, she had few friends. When she heard people approaching, she would pull herself up tremulously, hobble to the end of the porch, and perch querulously on her make shift walking stick: "*Pa passai isi la. Sa sai teh mwen,*" she would cry, saying, "Don't pass here. This is my land," in Creole. To be honest, it was a public path. There was no other way to access the homes at the rear. The adults largely ignored her, but the children were scared of her shouting and would scurry rather than walk past. The fact is, aside from her irascible ways, rumour had it that Ma Ivy was a *soucouyan,* that is, a witch.

I don't know about witches in other countries, but Dominican witches were scary. They were supposed to remove their skin to fly around at night and suck your blood while you slept. They were invisible except for their flickering light, but crafty villagers could catch them. The secret was to hang on to them until daylight, when they would revert to their earthly form, revealing their identity. Soucouyans sometimes left puncture marks on the skin or a trail of blood on your sheets, in clumsy remembrance of their visit. But without fail, the next morning, they would seek you out to have a conversation. That was another sure way to identify them. The main antiwitch remedy was garlic, soap, or sand placed underneath your bed or sticks placed in the form of a cross somewhere in your bedroom—which reminds me, you could also sleep with your clothes turned inside out. If children didn't do well at school, it was surely because their intelligence had been siphoned away while they slept. Ma Ivy was allegedly responsible for many such evils in her neighbourhood; no wonder most people were afraid of her.

But she wasn't alone—the village was awash with stories. Ma Gladys, for example, was a woman who never left her house. I caught sight of her a few times as a child when she peered through her curtains. I remember that she had curly black hair and pasty-white skin. We were terrified of going past her house and sprinted blindly for fear of being caught. The story was that she went out "hunting" one night and left her skin behind. The man who lived with her at that time got up and put pepper all over the skin and went back to sleep. When Ma Gladys returned and put her skin back on, the pepper burnt her all over. Since then, she never left her house. The thing is, we all believed that story as children, but now I wondered if the poor woman had had skin cancer or something.

My young friend, Malcolm, was another villager who was said to have had an encounter with *obeah*, only, in Dominica, we said *piaye*, not *obeah*. He had one normal leg and another enormous leg with bulbous lumps, which he dragged about laboriously. It was said that he had stepped on some powder placed by a jealous neighbour outside his mum's house, which had caused his leg to grow to its gigantic size.

"The boy has elephantiasis," my stepdad had said. I had never heard that word before, and the villagers' version was easier to believe, so I believed it. Then, life was simply divided into good or evil. We believed in God and the devil. All good things came from God, and bad things from the devil. Only, I have known a few devils in my time, and none of them has horns. Instead, they wear trousers and abuse women and children. Sometimes, hell, it seems, is right here on earth. Now, it looked like I had sold my soul to Lennox, the devil incarnate.

Chapter 6

As surely as good triumphs over evil, I triumphed over Lennox. Hurricane Drake, which wrought such havoc, changed the course of my life. Slowly, it dawned on me that the cycle of hatred and pain which had controlled me up to then had been broken. It seemed that I had left the bitterness of the past in Lennox's arms. I entered a new era of peace. I simply couldn't summon the resentment or anger required to plot revenge. I no longer wanted Lennox destroyed or dead. I just wanted peace.

I'm sorry to say that I didn't attend Susan's funeral. The police came to find me at my godmother's and took a statement. I told them all I knew, including about the bite marks and bruises that Susan had shown me. I felt that I owed her that much. She had obviously chosen death for herself and her child rather than a life of abuse and disregard with Lennox. I didn't feel the need to protect him. Plus, the evidence would be there for all to see.

But the villagers did start gossiping after the funeral. I heard the neighbours talking about Teacher Lennox's wife.

"Did you know he used to beat her?"

"She was like a prisoner; she couldn't go out."

"Dey say her father send her a ticket, but Lennox doh let her go back America."

I knew this last to be fantasy, because Susan had told me herself that she was an orphan. But that was the way of the village; we just fabricated what we weren't sure of. The ladies from Susan's church prepared her body and arranged the flowers for her funeral. They also arranged for the pastor of another church to bury her. From what I heard, Lennox went along but sat alone, weeping silently. He was given no role in the service and was not acknowledged in any way. The swarm of ladies who had followed and supported him as their pastor broke away and, instead, cared for Susan in her death. They sent her and her child off with love and dignity, but Lennox stood alone.

Myself, I was stuck in limbo. My days revolved endlessly around survival and caring for Ma Ivy—cooking and cleaning, drying out her possessions which had been soaked through by the hurricane. I used the opportunity to covertly get rid of the myriad of bric-a-brac she had accumulated over the years. But the hardest thing about the post hurricane days was dealing with bodily functions. We were forced to use a chamber pot since the shell of the outside pit toilet was completely gone. Only the raised concrete seat remained, like a cold, sad throne. It was still functional if one didn't mind easing oneself in full view of the neighbours, which, of course, I had been forced to do as a child. My dad's mum, Sonia, had had a prototype flushing toilet. It looked just like a normal toilet but required a bucket for flushing. A huge pipe conducted the waste to a pit dug some distance from the house. Of course, that beauty was reserved for the adults. We kids were relegated to using a hole cut in the waste pipe and squatted there in full view of passersby. I don't remember feeling any embarrassment, just discomfort at the smell and awkward posture. That's just how things were.

My clothes were still at Lennox's, so I wore Ma Ivy's. Around the house, I wore her long, shapeless dresses, but to go farther afield, I wore my jeans and gathered the dress in a knot at the hip. Everything was growing tight. I hardly ate anything, but I was spilling all over. My whole image was changing. I started growing my hair again, nurturing it with cactus shampoo and castor oil. I was blooming and happy, wishing my carefree days would never end.

Even going to the relief centre to collect supplies became an adventure. That was distributed from the old school building in the bay at the foot of the village. It was a good hour's walk from Ma Ivy's house. Salisbury was a long, winding village, like an elongated eel or snake, with houses on either side of a solitary road. The lower part was known simply as Salisbury or Lower Salisbury, the middle as La Savanne, and the topmost part as Tapi Veh, which sounds like the French for "green carpet." Each part of the village had a tempo and identity of its own. People from La Savanne thought their neighbours from Lower Salisbury were ill mannered and lazy. Certainly, there was more poverty and petty crime in that part of the village. In those days, pupils from La Savanne were more likely to go to secondry school and on to further education than were their counterparts from Lower Salisbury.

Tapi Veh seemed to grow out of the dust, an inevitable result of expansion and the economic buoyancy of the newly educated. More people were going to secondary school and abroad to university; therefore, more people had jobs in Roseau, the capital. Minibuses made the fourteen-mile trip there every morning, ferrying workers and students. Buses were all privately owned, but the government set the bus fare for all routes. Commuters liked their music loud and current and their drivers fast. Drivers gained nicknames like "Flying Pig" or "Best I Walk," depending on whether their passengers' thirst for speed was assuaged or not.

Sometimes, I caught the bus down to the Bay. Mostly, though, I walked. It was a chance to see long-lost friends and relatives. We all seemed to be related to each other in Salisbury. Whether by fact or fiction, everyone was "cousin." Sometimes, I would be stopped by an ageing adult enquiring imperiously, "*Ki moun ki mama'w?*"— Who is your mother?

"Agatha," I would respond. "*Zanfan Urma*"—Urma's child.

"Agatha? *Papa Agatha sai fweh papa mwen.*" Agatha's father is my father's brother.

I welcomed such interruptions. I had been away for so long and had spent so much time in my private world of twisted memories that I needed to bond with these warm people. They were my path to recovery and stability. But not everyone from abroad was welcomed unreservedly. You had to prove yourself, somewhat: project an image which was successful but not too successful, dress smartly but not extravagantly. No airs or graces, no posh English or American accents. Make eye contact and say hello first. Then, you would be celebrated, and the generosity of the villagers would be boundless.

One day, about midday, I set off for our rations, in the sweltering heat. I wore Ma Ivy's straw hat. The village stank a bit, like rancid clothes and half-rotting food. All was quiet, with just a few people milling about. We were subdued. Not expectant, just subdued. I was walking past a cousin's bakery off the playing field, when I heard my name called from inside.

"Miss Agnes, Miss Agnes!"

I didn't recognize the woman at first, but it was Ruthina, the maid from the hotel where I had stayed on arrival. Ruthina, out of uniform, was a tall, slim woman, still pale and freckled with bright red hair, but with a calm confidence which hadn't been visible at work. Two of her children were with her, little girls who looked just liked their mum.

"Ruthina, how are you girl?"

"I OK, Miss Agnes. You still here then? You was here for the hurricane?"

"Yes, I'm staying by Ma Ivy, my godmother."

"Oh, so Ma Ivy is your *nenen*?" Nenen was the colloquial term for godmother. "I didn't know dat. Dat lady so bad…"

Ruthina's intonation rose slightly at the end of every utterance in typical Dominican fashion. Her voice hovered like a question mark but showed not uncertainty, but relish. Ma Ivy's reputation was far-reaching, it seemed. But I didn't want the villagers finding out I had spent the night of the hurricane at Lennox's, so I deliberately led Ruthina to believe I had been at my godmother's. I didn't want to start a conversation about Susan's death, either. Instead, I asked Ruthina about herself and her family. She too was heading for the Bay and we walked slowly together. She also had two older boys who lived with their dad and paternal grandmother, leaving Ruthina free to start a relationship with the man who became her girls' dad. They weren't married but lived together in a small two-roomed house up in Tapi Veh.

"Who looks after your girls when you're at work, Ruthina?"

"My mother. She does bathe them for me and take them to school."

"What about their dad? What work does he do?"

"He's a policeman. He working St. Joseph. He staying there in di week, and he does come home at the weekend."

It looked like Ruthina's partner, Peter, was a raunchy lad. Two years her junior, he had fathered four other children in the village and another two in St. Joseph. All by different mums. But that wasn't unusual. Policemen were a great favourite of the ladies, and since they were frequently posted to different villages, they did spread their seed around.

Didn't she mind any of this?

"What can I do Miss Agnes? That's how he is. Those girls like him. They not giving him a chance."

I thought for a while about Ruthina's situation. Very representative of the life of a typical village girl. Men were frequently unfaithful and shied away from commitment, fathering children by different women as they exercised their virility. Worse still if you didn't have an education or job and were at their mercy financially. I don't think I had missed much by moving away. But I sensed that some things were changing. There were more marriages now among the younger generation than among their parents, but fidelity was frequently a fleeting concept.

Ruthina and I parted company when we got to the Bay. She met some of her friends but I just wanted to be alone for a while to touch base with my inner self and evaluate my situation. By now, I had been in Dominica for a few months. It had been at least two since the hurricane struck. But I had changed. From inside. I had to find out who this new Agnes was and what she wanted from me and from life. What were her plans? Was she going to remain in Dominica or return to Britain? I had no idea. I strolled around pensively, looking at the devastation. The coconut grove, which had been my classroom as a child, was completely flattened. Not one coconut palm remained standing. But they would grow back because every coconut was potentially another palm. They would sprout eventually, take root in the rich soil and grow anew into tall, majestic sentinels.

The roof had been blown off the old school, but children played hide-and-seek among the partitioned walls while they waited for their queuing parents. I was surprised to see that the old toilet was still standing. More of a shed, really. A shed with a bucket. It smelled less offensive than I remembered. I peered gingerly around the door hanging lopsidedly. There was no bucket inside anymore, just the exposed planks of the floor. And a freshly deposited human loaf in a corner. I beat a hasty retreat and headed for the sea.

The beach was completely covered in gravel. The black sand had been washed away. Gravel, seaweed and driftwood were the new occupants. Apart from two beaches in the north of the island, Dominica's beaches were all black sand, reflecting its volcanic origins. I guess tourists would find that strange, but it did add to the old-worldiness of the place. I turned right opposite the jetty and started towards the rocks at the far end of that section of the bay, picking up a few shells as I went along. But I didn't keep them. I just looked at their intricate patterns and delicate pink underbellies and dropped them again. I was restless. I felt strangely irritable, but there was nothing wrong. No one had bothered me or tried to ruin my day. It was just me. Ma Ivy's dress was pulled tight across my chest, pressing my breasts into a mushy mass. That was perhaps the source of my discomfort. And that strange, metallic taste in my mouth. It was there all the time, and I couldn't get rid of it. I wondered if it was just the taste of the boiled stream water we were obliged to drink since Hurricane Drake.

There was a male figure up ahead sitting on one of the rocks and looking out to sea. I made a mental note to stop before I got to him and to return to the bustle of the main bay. Up ahead, the man must have caught sight of me from the corner of his eye, because he seemed to do a double-take. He stood slowly. As he unfolded his seated form, he raised the brim of his cap which was half-hiding his features. I noticed first his white spotted beard and then his brown eyes. He looked straight at me, steadily, not smiling; just looking. Almost daring me to turn away. I took a deep breath and came up to him. My heart beat erratically like a trapped winged creature. My knees trembled slightly as I approached, and I just seemed to fall into his arms. His lips searched for mine, but I turned away instinctively and pulled back slowly.

"Hi, Lennox," I said.

"Agnes."

It was more of a sigh than a whisper. Or maybe, more of a whimper, a longing. Still needing me to be close, he held on to my arm tightly as I moved away from him. I looked at Lennox squarely, determined to find out once and for all who he was. Was he good or evil? He seemed to need me. Was it me or just any woman? Could I trust him? Believe in him? Who was he?

"Agnes, I need to talk to you." He was pleading with his eyes, but his tone was neutral. No precursor to the bombshell which was to follow.

I looked at him enquiringly. "My clothes are still at your place," I said. "How can I get them?"

"Agnes, I, um"—he looked suddenly uncomfortable—"I can take you there now," he finished rather quickly.

I nodded silently, and he kept hold of my hand, leading me in the direction from which I had come. I was a little uncomfortable about being seen strolling hand in hand with Lennox. Not that he wasn't presentable or anything. He was a good-looking man, but I don't think he was popular in the village then, after his treatment of Susan. I didn't want anyone thinking that I had taken her place. But Lennox's hand was warm and comforting. I still liked his smell, and his eyes, and his teeth. And his short, speckled beard. And his smile. And his strong, soothing voice. You know what? I think I rather fancied him! Under different circumstances, I wouldn't have thought twice about it. But I knew too much, knew him too well. Apart from his despicable act towards me as a child, I had seen the marks on Susan's body. I was wise enough to know that if he had treated her that violently, it would only be a matter of time before he became disenchanted with me and subjected me to the same. I loved myself. I had resolved long ago never to knowingly put myself in a situation of potential abuse.

Lennox didn't say much on the way to his house. I said even less. We travelled in his pick-up truck to Ti Tanse, which really wasn't that far away. I asked him how he managed to procure petrol since the hurricane. He laughed and said that he had his contacts. There were very few vehicles on the road since that fateful day. Most of the roads still hadn't been cleared of fallen trees and landslides. Lennox entertained me with a few stories about looting and fights breaking out at the relief distribution centre, and before I knew it, we had turned into the stony road leading to his house. The home he'd shared with Susan. The house where I'd lived through the hurricane. The house where I had given myself to him. The house that I'd left in disquiet, the morning after. I didn't know if I could bear to return.

Chapter 7

I was back at my mum's. In characteristic style, she had summoned my presence. My brother had arrived early one morning, saying, "Mammy say is time to come home."

So I obeyed. When I got home, her greeting was frosty.

"You putting on weight! Look at your taytay"—breasts—"bursting in that top!"

I hadn't seen my mum since before the hurricane, but my brother had made regular trips to Ma Ivy's, checking on me and relaying information to my mum. The first bulletin concerned where and how I had survived the hurricane. "At Lennox's," I said. When he returned a few days later, there was a new question: "Mammy say, if you were there when Susan die."

"Yes, but I don't want to talk about it," I replied.

To be honest, I was only that brave because my mum wasn't present. I wouldn't have dared say that to her face. I know that I needed to be stronger with her, stand up for myself more. I could only do that with strangers, though. I was still like a child in my mother's presence. When I was growing up, adults ruled, and children bowed. Anyone could reprimand you, not just your parents. Not saying hello to an adult was a serious offence. My mum was like a bulldozer. She could cut right through your feelings as she aired her dissatisfaction with your partner, morals, job, etiquette… She just didn't give one the opportunity to fight back. So, still, I fell in line.

My mum's comment about my weight irked a bit. I was aware that I was gaining weight. Only, I didn't know why. I hardly ate anything. I wasn't even interested in Ma Ivy's cooking when I was in Salisbury. And Ma Ivy always cooked the most wonderful dishes. Normally, I couldn't resist her soup. The aroma of smoked pork as it cooked slowly with pigeon peas was enough to get an anorexic begging. Ma Ivy smoked the pork herself in the yard, on a makeshift wire stand. Green saplings provided a steady supply of smoke, and, broad green leaves imparted a special flavour to the meat. Since she didn't own a stove, Ma Ivy cooked her soup slowly over an open fire, adding pumpkin and *tania* yams, along with dumplings and green bananas. It really was a treat. But the last time she made her soup, I left it untouched. The very smell put me off. I was a little worried now. Was I ill or something? Maybe I had caught a tummy bug? I wasn't sure how to get to a doctor. Going to Roseau was a tortuous business. At least two bridges had collapsed along the way, and there were still landslides blocking the road in Tarreau and Rockaway. Whole cliffs had caved in. Mero, where my mum lived, was the next village on from Salisbury, and the commute was still possible. So, the journey back home had been relatively straightforward.

My mum wanted to know about the night when Susan died. She heard that Susan had committed suicide; was that right?

"I don't know," I answered sourly.

"So where you sleep after she die?"

Next very difficult question. My mum was shrewd; she understood unspoken things. She had tried to picture Susan's death in her mind's eye and couldn't place my whereabouts. That bothered her. Well, I was not going to confess to spending the night in Lennox's arms.

"Mum, Susan is dead. Please let her rest in peace," was my convenient response.

That bought me some time, and I disappeared quickly into the sanctuary of my bedroom. I caught sight of myself in the mirror and stopped, shocked. I hadn't actually looked in a mirror since the hurricane. There were no mirrors in Ma Ivy's house. My hair had grown and was at that difficult, in-between stage: too long to be cute and too short to do anything decent with. So I oiled it and left it loose, like a shaggy dog. But it was my breasts which were the greatest surprise. They literally seemed to burst through my top. My jeans were obviously too small. I had to suck in my stomach to do up the buttons, and my flab just hung there in a desperate roll. I looked all wrong. Not like the sleek, sophisticated woman who had landed all those months ago. I had to change that.

Apart from a few sheets of galvanize roofing which had been torn off in the hurricane, my mum's house was intact. My clothes were exactly where I had left them, and I rummaged to find a loose cotton top. I combed my hair and put on some lip gloss. But, to be honest, I had a bigger problem: Lennox had asked me to marry him.

As we approached his house that day, my heart had begun thumping in my chest. I squirmed anxiously in my seat and reached for Lennox's arm on the steering wheel.

"Lennox, I can't. Please, I can't," I had been panic-stricken. I couldn't go back to that awful house.

"Agnes, please. I need you to come with me."

"Lennox, please take me back. Please stop. *Lennox!*" I was screaming then, my eyes blind with imagined fears.

Lennox had stopped the truck and looked at me. "Agnes, I really need you to come with me. I'm at breaking point. Everyone has deserted me. Please, Agnes, I need your help."

The sound of Lennox begging me for support calmed my fear, and I turned and looked at him. He looked sad and desperate, and a flicker of pity stirred in my breast. I had never ever felt anything but resentment for Lennox. Later, a twisted attraction, but never empathy. I relented. We continued and Lennox stopped outside what was left of his house. I tried not to look around. My heart was aching with actual, physical pain. My breathing was short and sharp. The memories of that night spent cowering in the hurricane and of Susan's gory death came flooding back. I was glued to my seat. Lennox seemed to be having trouble as well. He too remained seated and turned to me.

"Agnes, I know that I've not been the best that I could be. I've made a lot of mistakes. I would like us to try again."

"Try what again?" I had asked, genuinely confused.

"You know, us," he replied.

"Us? I'm not sure what you mean, Lennox."

He had looked slightly embarrassed. Maybe he hadn't expected me to press him like this. But I honestly wasn't sure what he was trying to say. Us? Did he want me to go out with him? Did he want us to be better friends?

I looked at him frankly, waiting for his explanation. If anything, he looked more embarrassed. He took a deep breath and I think he decided to dive straight in, because he said, "Agnes, I want to marry you."

"What?" I was aghast.

"I want to marry you!" He was shouting, almost. "I want to marry you, okay."

I was silent.

"What do you say to that?"

I can't explain the depth of my shock and final horror. Marry Lennox? Not even if he were the last man standing. A man who abused children and women? The worst sort of man ever? A true coward? No, I didn't think so. I turned to face him fully.

"Lennox, I can't marry you." Every word had been clear and crisp. "You've done too much. You've not even had the guts to say sorry for what you did to me. Look at Susan; she was covered in bruises. How can you expect me to marry you?"

His face had clouded progressively as I continued. By the time I had finished, it was a thundercloud. His eyebrows had puckered, and his eyes had hardened. The veins bulged in his neck, and he hunched over the steering wheel.

"That's the thing about you women; you can never let anything go. That's why I had to discipline Susan. She just wouldn't obey. Always arguing with me and trying to be difficult. I told you before, I never did anything to you. It's all in your head."

You know, Lennox was nothing to me. Susan was also dead. I didn't need to reason with him. I just wanted him out of my life.

"Lennox, please, can I just get my stuff from your home, and then I'll leave, okay?"

"Yes, dey just inside where you leff them."

Like all educated Dominicans, Lennox circulated within the three language systems at his disposal, preferring, however, to stick to a mixture of Standard English and the more loosely constructed vernacular. My decoding it was automatic, as if he had only used one variety.

However, I couldn't bear to go in, and I had asked him if he would mind getting them for me. He snorted impatiently, but got out nonetheless. Less than five minutes later, he was back, carrying my travel bag and a couple of plastic shopping bags with odds and ends. I had thanked him but said nothing more. There was nothing else to be said. I just wanted to be free of Lennox King forever.

So now, I lay there on my bed at my mum's, musing on the past and on Lennox's proposal. Could I have married him? Had I done the right thing by refusing? Did I care for him in any way? I did like Lennox. And I did feel attracted to him. Based on just physical attraction, I could have had a relationship with him. But a man was more than the sum of his physique. At my age, I was looking for integrity and character. No, I didn't think I had made a mistake. So, I lay there on my bed at my mum's, happy to put Lennox and the past to rest.

I was drifting off when he started his crusade. No, not Lennox; Terrence, the guy who lived next door. His house was so close that I could smell his unwashed body from my bedroom. He smelled like a ram. Terrence was the bane of the neighbourhood and of my mum's household. Most of the neighbours said that he wasn't mad, "just wicked." In any case, about twice a week, he would have a physical fight with his demons. He had just started as I was drifting off. Most of it happened in Creole, but he switched sometimes depending on which of his personas was talking. Terrence invented the most terrible swear words ever. They were long and complicated and involved slowly and methodically deconstructing the female anatomy—with maternal reference. I wondered if he were really possessed by demons. How else could he say such terrible things?

Terrence went through his act in different voices. First, he was one person, then another. Sometimes he was female and spoke in a high-pitched, affected voice; then he would respond in deep masculine tones. His efforts really were worthy of Hollywood. It was hard not to laugh as he spoke to his invisible friends:

"You ready for me? You ready for me?"—You want a fight, do you?

"Me pardner, I doh care with you, you know. I just checking my scene"—I'm just minding my business.

"You fink I 'fraid you. Man, I slamming you, wi?"— Do you want a thump from me?

This was followed by a high-pitched feminine shriek and the most awful banging and slamming like a gang of people engaged in a fight. Only, by then, I knew that it was probably only Terrence at home. I used to think that the house was full of people, and I'd be terrified when the banging and slamming began. So, one day, I peered through the curtains, trying to make out the shapes in the gloom of his kitchen. He was alone, running to and fro, waving a stick, and hitting out indiscriminately. The neighbours had got the police to take away his cutlass after he had threatened some of the children. "I going to kill a *chile*"—child—"tonight," he would promise each time they went past. Since no one could be sure that he wouldn't, his cutlass was taken away. Even before the hurricane, his house resembled a bombed out shell in a war zone. He had already removed all the windows and doors and had ripped off his toilet and kitchen units. The only work left was for the hurricane to remove the roof. Instead, it passed safely through the other convenient openings and left the roof intact. Actually, it probably did him a favour by blowing all his garbage away. Since he had no toilet, Terrence invented an innovative way of easing himself—he defecated in plastic bags and flung them out into his front yard. I tell you, Terrence tested his neighbours' Christian spirit to the limit.

But maybe he could be excused for his behaviour? Terrence was an orphan. His mum, Thelma, had drowned while trying to cross a swollen river after some heavy rainfall. His sister Abigail, who was disabled and had two stumps for hands, looked on in horror, unable to help her mum as she grappled and struggled to regain her footing. Abigail screamed and called desperately for help, but by the time a workman arrived from a nearby distillery, Thelma had long disappeared. Terrible experience for the kids and neighbours. Thelma was actually from one of the neighbouring islands, and so, her children had no other relatives in Dominica. Abigail had been about sixteen when their mum died, and Terrence had been fourteen. Abigail, though, was quite independent, having had to fend for herself and her brother while their mum earned a living. She did the laundry, cooking, and cleaning. Her mum left her another property in a nearby village, while Terrence inherited the house next to my Mum's. Abigail had married at eighteen. A pharmacist from Nigeria living and working in St. Joseph had whisked her off. Everyone thought that he just wanted an opportunity to remain in Dominica and expand his prospects. I heard all of that through the grapevine, of course. Terrence and Abigail were just children when I left Dominica. She stopped by to visit me at my mum's, and I was pleasantly surprised to find she had grown into a full-figured, lovely woman. She had two children and said that she was happy. Her husband loved her and treated her well, she said. The villagers must have been wrong, then. Or were they? Women all over the world were protecting their men.

But I felt sad for Terrence. The fact was, apart from offering him the occasional meal, we all just left him to his own devices. I thought about what a generous woman his mother had been and wondered if she really could be looking down at Terrence, shocked and grieved by the fact that her son had been reduced to living like an animal. I mean, when we die, do we really go to heaven, hell or purgatory? Not that I have ever seen any evidence for purgatory in the bible. Do our loved ones really look down at us, cringing as we bungle our lives—the way they had theirs, perhaps? All this religious stuff was above my head. I believed in God, but more out of habit than anything else. I mean, no one had ever seen him. But, on the other hand, was earth the big accident that scientists proposed? To be honest, sometimes it took as much faith to believe in certain scientific theories as it did to believe in God. Try as I might, I couldn't see how life could start from nothing. I mean *nothing*; that is, before the bits of energy, minerals, and proteins collided to start a chain reaction. Where did the first spark of life come from? Secondly, an asteroid supposedly dropped from the sky and wiped out the dinosaurs—but nothing else. I would have expected such a destructive asteroid to have wrecked the planet a bit more and not so selectively. And why haven't we had a similarly destructive one since? In my view, conjecture for conjecture, an all-knowing, all-powerful, invisible God didn't seem that far-fetched. Plus, the other thing that haunted me was my experience in Lennox's church. No one had been physically touching me when I fell to the floor. Just a strong force in the pit of my stomach, which floored me. I couldn't have stopped myself from falling. And that sense of peace that overshadowed me was no figment of my imagination.

I pondered and must have fallen asleep because I had a strange dream. Zena, a young friend of mine in London, came up to me and offered me a present. It was two lots of outfits for a baby boy. I can still see them lying there—tiny pale blue shirts with delicate lace edging and matching bootees. I woke with a start, anxious, wondering what it could mean. But I told no one of my dream.

Chapter 8

The next morning, my neighbour, Shirley, dropped by unexpectedly. Her niece was getting married at the weekend, and she wondered if I would like to accompany her to the ceremony. It was going to be a Creole wedding, and Shirley thought I might enjoy it. I was touched. Yes, I would certainly enjoy it, I assured her. A chance to revel in our culture and eat my favourite foods—not to be missed without a good reason. We set out early on the Saturday for Massacre, pronounced, *massak*, where the wedding was being held. Massacre was a small village on the way to Roseau, not far from Canefield. I hadn't been farther than St. Joseph since the hurricane. I had only heard about the state of the roads, and I wasn't looking forward to the journey. Also, I wasn't happy with my outfit. It just wasn't wedding-like. I didn't know why I was gaining weight when I hardly ate anything. I sighed and settled for the most decent thing that fitted: loose khaki trousers and a soft red top. I wrapped a red madras scarf around my head in recognition of the Creole theme. But I was still half asleep as I got dressed. I was quite tempted to change my mind and go back to bed, but it would mean Shirley going alone. Shirley was in her fifties and childless. She had been a matron at the hospital in Roseau for many years, but had taken early retirement because of ill health. I was sure she'd asked me for the companionship, and it wouldn't have been nice to pull out at the last minute. So, I did my neighbourly duty.

Shirley didn't drive, therefore, we hitchhiked to Massacre. Normally, that wouldn't have been too difficult, but Shirley had a huge pot of black pudding carrying to the wedding and there were necessarily fewer vehicles on the road since the hurricane. So, we started walking towards St. Joseph, staying initially along the inner road of the village itself and exiting next to the Castaways Hotel. To be honest, I wasn't happy when my mum moved to Mero after leaving my stepdad. I would have preferred to have gone somewhere more exciting like Canefield or Goodwill. Mero was just a very sleepy hamlet: crescent-shaped with a playing field, a few bars and grocery shops, but not much else. No school. But there was a lovely beach right next to the solitary road traversing the settlement. You could step right off the road and unto the beach. But all of that got washed up during the hurricane. We made our way slowly across boulders and broken tarmacadam, jumping and sidestepping to avoid the encroaching sea. The Castaways Hotel was there, just outside of Mero. I peeked through the fronds of the battered palms and saw that it had taken a good lashing. It looked deserted. Just as we started up the hill, we heard the sound of an engine, and Shirley flagged down the grey truck which came along. There was a couple at the front, but the driver stopped anyway, and we hoisted ourselves up at the back. I just took a deep breath and braced myself for the crazy drive. But the driver moved at the pace of a funeral march. The truck laboured up the steep hill unto St. Joseph. Shirley laughed, saying that we would have been better off running alongside. We went through the village of St. Joseph, and the old man stopped abruptly. He blew his horn to attract our attention and beckoned impatiently for us to get off. He was turning into his driveway and wanted us off. I looked at him for a second and did a double take. He looked strangely familiar. A small, grey-haired man with a straight nose and freckles. A younger woman cradling a small dog sat next to him. It was spooky, how familiar he looked, but Shirley called and I jumped off, leaving my thoughts. I never found out who he was.

The journey to the wedding didn't get any more exciting, except for having to negotiate the river at Layou to get to the other side. And crawling over a few slides on the way. I thought bitterly that the food had better be good when we got there. It had taken us two hours to get to Massacre. A journey of about twenty-five minutes at the best of times. But as we got off the main road and started up the steep hill to the church, I felt the first buzz of excitement. The church was an imposing building standing in stark isolation at the top of a long, concrete path. Small gravestones lined the precarious path, as if keeping a chilly watch on the besotted pilgrims who plodded up, anxious for redemption and grace. I wondered idly what would happen if those graves unexpected opened as the wedding guests passed by, spilling their ghoulish contents. The main cemetery actually lay beneath the road leading to Roseau, right at the top of a sheer cliff leading to the foaming sea below. It was a wonder that the mourners and their dearly departed didn't roll off during the funeral ceremony.

It occurred to me that I still didn't know whose wedding I was going to. I knew Shirley only as my mum's neighbour, and I hadn't met any of her relatives. But I was touched that she had invited me. We hadn't spoken much along the way, concentrating our energies on negotiating the tricky route. The steep road leading to the church was crammed tight with vehicles, some of them very expensive. It looked like an important wedding. I thought again that I might not be suitably dressed. But then, there had just been a serious hurricane; surely expectations were lowered to reflect this? Maybe not, by the look of some of the cars. As we approached, I could see that a large tarpaulin had been stretched across the courtyard of the church, forming a sort of makeshift shelter in inevitable anticipation of the sun's scorching rays. It looked like the reception was going to held right there in the yard. Tables and chairs were set out in neat rows, with a few tables laid across one length, brimming with covered dishes and pots. Strangely though, there was hardly anyone around. Just two ladies fussing with lids and paper plates. Shirley unloaded her burden of black pudding and asked one of them, "We late, non?"

"Not really, di groom inside, but we still waiting for di bride. You have time."

"OK, let me just straighten up"

I hadn't paid attention to Shirley's outfit before. She was wearing a loose dress over her Creole costume, and as I watched, she pulled a *moushweh*—madras scarf, which sounds like French for handkerchief—out of her bag and draped it expertly around her head. A quick smooth of her madras skirt and we headed indoors. The church was packed. I wondered that we hadn't heard the noise from outside. People weren't waiting quietly. They talked and called out to each other, complaining about the bride's tardiness. Children ran about, dodging in and out of pews. The priest was nowhere in sight, and certainly, I couldn't see the groom. I followed Shirley as she butted her way to the far corner of the rear pew. I had no idea what time it was. I guessed about eight thirty in the morning, based on the time we had left Mero. I felt suddenly hungry. Shirley had turned up just before six, and I hadn't eaten anything. Then, there was this dull ache in the centre of my back. I wondered if I had pulled a muscle climbing over mounds of earth and rocks on the way. I couldn't wait for it all to be over so I could eat. Shirley made herself comfortable, but didn't talk to anyone. Instead, she kept craning her neck towards the door, as if willing her niece to arrive. I too settled down to wait.

It wasn't long before the priest strode in via one of the side entrances. Two suited men at the front stood up abruptly as he did. They were just vague outlines to me. I could hardly see what was going on from that distance. The sound of a car pulling up outside pierced into the general cacophony within the church, and a sudden hush descended on the waiting congregation. "She's here," Shirley whispered to me, and we turned, in unison, towards the entrance of the church, eager for the first glimpse of the bride.

But it was another five minutes before anyone appeared through the doorway. Two little flower girls and their pages trouped slowly in, wearing traditional clothing. The girls wore long madras skirts and white frilly cotton tops with the obligatory madras moushweh of the national dress. Their lips were crudely made up with bright red lipstick which was also used as rouge in wide circles on their cheeks, rather like the red circles on a clown's cheek. Only it didn't look out of place, because that exaggerated makeup was itself part of the costume. The girls also wore large, gold-coloured necklaces and each carried a small basket of anthurium lilies. The boys were demurely dressed in black trousers and a white shirt, with a black bow tie at the neck and a red sash at the waist.

As they appeared in the doorway, the organist began the bridal march, and the children started slowly down the aisle in an uncoordinated bunch. Then, the bride herself floated into view. There was a collective gasp. She wore the full *dwiyet* dress, only, instead of the madras patterns of the guests, her gown was in glorious white: A tight, long-sleeved, fitted bodice which flared dramatically at the waist into a full skirt made with yards and yards of patterned silk. It was gathered at intervals across the hips, so that it rose and fell all around in a sort of jagged- edged pattern. A white cotton petticoat peeped flirtatiously from underneath, with a slash of gold ribbon threaded through eyelets at the bottom. The gold was mirrored exactly by plain gold pumps. It was astoundingly simple, yet so extravagantly Creole. She posed theatrically in the doorway with a bouquet of white lilies and the folds of her skirt draped over her arm.

The bride was definitely in her element, soaking up the attention offered by her guests. She beamed as we admired her, revealing a small gap in her teeth. Gold accessories flashed as she started her slow march: a gold-coloured scarf draped loosely around her neck and knotted at her breast with a giant brooch. Simple gold earrings and then the piece de resistance—her madras headdress. I had never seen that shade of madras before, and I wondered if she had made a special trip to Martinique or Guadeloupe to find something different. It was white and gold striped cotton, with hints of red and green reflected here and there in thin, almost imperceptible lines. Starched rigid into the shape of a sort of low hat, it finished strikingly with three peaks in the middle. Other women in the church had various versions of the headdress—some fan-shaped or with one, two, or four peaks. Apparently, in the old days, the peaks were supposed to indicate a woman's marital status: one said that she was free; two, that she was taken but still open; and four, that she was available to all who desired her. The bride's three peaks said that her heart was fully engaged. I smiled as I watched her glide past our pew, and wondered how long her state of blissful happiness would last. I believed in love, but marriage seemed like an impossible union. Maybe men and women were not designed to physically live in the same space. I mean, in many primitive cultures, the sexes appeared to have lived separately, coming together specifically to procreate. I wondered if marriages would fare better if men and women didn't actually live together, stifling each other under a mound of unrealistic expectations. But every bride opted for the fairy tale of romantic love, expecting her beloved to bestow on her the adulation her heart whispered that she deserved. No wonder so many dreams ended in dust. My own dreams had been shattered while I was too young to know.

I watched bemused as the bride swayed joyfully towards her unenviable meeting with destiny. She was already halfway down the aisle when I noticed that the organ had given way to a local *jing-ping* sound. Instead of playing the bridal march, the musicians were shaking traditional *shakshak* rattles and beating hard on drums. It was hypnotic. Almost imperious. The drums seemed to be thrashing out a sinister mix calculated to drag the bride and her party to their peril. Red and green madras peaks bobbed and quivered all around the church in time to the music, as if their owners suffered from a severe case of ague. But it all became too much for me. As I watched, the peaks all melted into one, and I felt the corrosive edge of bile rising in my throat. It was hot and stifling, and I was definitely going to be sick. As the sensation permeated my upper body, I got up quickly, grunting apologetically as I scrambled over outstretched knees and ankles, in an undignified bid for the door. I just made it to some bushes at the side of the church, where I was violently, yet refreshingly sick. Not a very promising start to an exciting event. I stayed outside in the blessed fresh air and missed the Creole wedding of the century.

Chapter 9

My friend, Marcia, whom I had met in Roseau the day after my arrival, turned up unexpectedly, not long after the wedding. I was asleep. I seemed to sleep all the time. I wasn't sure if I was ill or if my subconscious was trying to escape from the thoughts and images that plagued my every waking moment. I was in the throes of a most formidable dilemma: what to do about what happened at the wedding. Should I have done something? Should I have told Shirley? Was it too late? Would I be responsible for wrecking even more lives? I tossed erratically at night and slept in the daytime when I should have been awake and productive. To this day, I am still tormented by what unfolded at the wedding, and I have never shared the details with anyone. Maybe the time has come to tell the world.

That day in Massacre, after rushing out of the marriage ceremony and being sick, I decided to remain outdoors. The thought of returning to the airless enclosure of the church was more than I could bear. Plus, I felt no obligation to witness the bride and groom exchange their vows—I had no idea who they were. The two ladies who were organising the buffet on our arrival were sat out in the courtyard, perspiring and fanning distractedly as they talked. I asked timidly if I could have some food. I wasn't sure how they would feel about me eating before the other guests. The older of the two looked up briefly and nodded before carrying on with her conversation. I wondered if they had heard me retching. I helped myself quickly and wandered off, eager to be alone before the rest of the wedding party emerged.

I followed a narrow path round the side of the church. The noise from inside sounded like bees buzzing, but it was mostly unintelligible. The grounds were steep and rocky, with little vegetation, mostly cacti and hibiscus interspersed with other local plants. The concrete path led unexpectedly to a small clearing, with a few benches set out around a minuscule pond. Tiny frogs, flies, and mosquitoes hopped, hovered, and fed, but there were no fish that I could see. In the far right corner was a small grotto featuring statues of the Holy Family. In the distance, to the left, was the ever-present Caribbean Sea, sparkling like a million sequins. The perfect representation of peace. I was drawn to the statue of Mary. There were so many stories of her appearing to ordinary people over the years. I wondered if they were true. And if they were, would she speak to me? I was desperate for a word about my life. Some guidance about the future; something or someone to mend the pieces of my life; make me whole again. But Mary stared past me in stony silence. I was left alone, as usual, with my pain.

I sat on the bench and finished my breakfast, reflecting on the vagaries of life – how easily our circumstances could change; how effortlessly the things we worked for could be snatched from us. There I was at a wedding – could I too be married soon? Would I meet my prince charming beside a stagnant pond with a few carved images as witnesses?

"Hello, stranger!"

I shrieked and turned around, expecting to find some insane creature waiting to devour me. Instead, I looked into a vaguely familiar, smiling face.

"Hi," I answered politely, not sure who he was. He was very tall, and, I suspect, appeared even taller because of my seated position, which meant that I had his protruding belly right at eye level.

He laughed, realizing that I hadn't recognised him. "So, Agnes, you don't remember me?"

I had to concede. "You look familiar, but I'm sorry, I don't know who you are. Are you from Salisbury?"

He moved closer and sat on the bench, next to me. "Agnes, I can't believe you've forgotten me. We had such good times together. I never forgot you, man."

Good times? Was my past coming back to haunt me? I made a greater effort to discern his features behind his gold-rimmed glasses. Maybe he hadn't worn those when I knew him? He was slightly cross-eyed and seemed to stare bizarrely at the bushes while smiling in my direction. An untidy moustache framed very pink lips, which puckered into a fleshy pout as he waited. I hesitated—I had only ever had one lover with pink lips. I gasped as recognition dawned. No!

"Nelson?" I whispered. He reached out and took my hand reassuringly. He looked softer than I remembered. Kinder, I should say. I hadn't thought about him in years, though. He had been married when I knew him, and we'd had a brief liaison which hadn't ended well. I certainly hadn't expected to see him again.

"How did you know I was here?" I asked him

"I saw you leave. I was just across from you in the church."

"Yeah, I wasn't feeling well. I just needed some fresh air."

He grinned mischievously. "Yes, I heard you being sick. That went quite well with the music."

"Oh no, how embarrassing! But how are you, Nelson? How's your family?"

His face fell. "My kids are all grown now. They've all migrated to the States."

"Oh, I see. And your wife, how is she?"

"She's not too well. Actually, Agnes, we're not expecting her to live for much longer."

I made to ask him something further when he interrupted.

"Agnes, look, I don't have much time. I need to get back in there. I just came out to give you a message."

"A message?" I was shocked.

"Yes, from God. He says it's time to come to him, time to stop running. He says that he's waiting for you."

I'm not sure how I felt after hearing that. Anger? Annoyance? Resentment? Another message from "God"! Is that all these people thought about? Here was another man who got religion after indulging his carnal desires. Had they forgotten their past? I opened my mouth to lecture Nelson and surprised myself by bursting into tears.

I didn't know why. I wasn't upset about anything in particular. I think the invitation to come home touched a raw cord in my heart. I ached to belong, to know that the God who had let me down during my childhood really cared for me. But why should I trust him now?

I felt that I should put the question to Nelson. Apart from Marcia, he was the only person who knew what happened to me as a child.

"So where was he then, Nelson, when I was a child? Why did he allow that man to rape me?" I was angry.

"Agnes," Nelson said patiently. "The bible refers to the devil as the 'prince of this world.' God is there looking down on us, but he doesn't intervene in our lives on a daily basis. We have to keep choosing good over evil. Every time someone chooses evil, that person causes another person pain."

"Right. But what about innocent children? Doesn't God have a duty of care towards them? A duty to keep them safe?"

"I agree, Agnes. But you need to know that God loves us all. Especially children. And ever time they hurt, he hurts. Jesus said that their angels constantly behold the face of God in heaven. I think we need to keep claiming his protection. You know, activate everything with faith."

"So, you're saying that if I have enough faith, nothing bad will ever happen to me?" I was sceptical. I knew many Christians who suffered excruciatingly.

"In theory, it should be like that, but it isn't. We're applying human logic to God. The bible says when Jesus returns as King, there'll be no more pain or suffering. Until then, God only appears to intervene sometimes to stop evil things."

"Well, I guess, I pulled the short straw, then." I was bitter about this 'God' who hadn't protected me in my innocence. I couldn't buy the message that he loved me.

"Agnes, you know, it's only the Spirit of God that can help us understand these things. Not our human wisdom."

Then, without asking for my permission, Nelson began praying for me. "Father, please help Agnes understand how much you love her. Touch her by the power of your Spirit. Let her understand beyond a shadow of a doubt, the height and breadth of your love. In Jesus name. Amen."

I was at peace.

"Agnes, I owe you an apology for what happened all those years ago." He looked deep into my eyes. Actually, he tried to. One eye seemed to while the other continued its crazy dance.

"You know, I loved you, but I shouldn't have gone out with you. I was married. I never thought of the pain I was causing both you and my wife."

I reached for Nelson and just hung on to him. His apology meant more to me than any preaching about God's love. Yes, maybe he was changed after all. Maybe this God thing worked. I wondered if I would ever get an apology from Lennox.

The church bell started tolling harshly, signalling the end of the wedding. Nelson and I straightened instinctively. "Girl, I have to go now. I have to. God bless you. Think about what I said, OK?"

I nodded. I opened my mouth to ask him something else, but he was already striding down the path. I wondered if I would ever get to know his God. Did God really exist, or was he just a figment of many people's imagination? But what if he really did exist? Would I let my pride keep me from knowing him? I didn't know then, that time would lead me very close to his throne.

"Agnes! Agnes! Come on, the wedding's over. Come and meet my niece."

I started. It was Shirley, of course, calling for me above the din of the wedding party. I was glad to be interrupted. This place, lonely and abandoned as it was, was beginning to get to me. I wondered if that meeting with Nelson had been a dream. Had I fallen asleep by the pond? I got up and started walking towards Shirley. My thoughts turned towards the bride whose wedding I'd missed. I felt a deep, unexplained sense of foreboding and I wondered what surprise awaited me at the end of the path.

∽

When Shirley called out to me, I dried my tears and straightened my clothes as I went. I felt suddenly shabby in my trousers and top. It hadn't mattered when I had got dressed in the early dawn, but now that the sun was out and sparkling on the garishly clad wedding guests, I felt dowdy. Shirley beckoned impatiently, and I hastened towards her. I wish I could have sat out the whole affair. But I had to be courteous, so I went to meet the bride. She smiled as we approached and opened her arms wide to receive her aunt. Then she turned towards me and smiled. She had a small gap in her teeth. Her makeup was immaculate, but she looked less interesting close up; more ordinary, I should say. Although I'd never met her, she looked familiar. I wondered if it were just a family resemblance to Shirley. I was about to ask her name, when her aunt cut in.

"Where's your husband? I haven't met him, you know."

The bride turned and pointed out her husband in the far corner. His back was to us, and he was surrounded by a group of guests. They seemed to be taking pictures. "Look, he over there. He and Anna." The groom was holding on to a little, curly-haired girl.

"Oh. That's your daughter? Boy, she looking nice. But I need to meet your husband. Where he from again?"

"Malta. I met him when I was studying."

I froze and looked again sharply at the young lady before me. No wonder she looked familiar—I had seen her photograph previously. I turned slowly to look back at the groom; willing him not to be who I thought he was. But he turned right at that moment, searching for his bride. Our eyes met. Mr. Ian Fenek. Trainee priest from Malta. Or, should I say, married lecturer from Malta. I didn't know which to believe any more. Ian did a double take as our eyes met, then, his eyes glazed over impersonally. He turned back to his daughter who was tugging at his trousers. Deeply shaken, I turned to his bride. "I'm sorry; I still don't know your name. I'm Agnes."

She smiled again, more widely this time. "I'm Patsy."

"And your husband, what's his name?"

"Ian. He's from Malta. That's our daughter with him."

"Yes, I..." I stopped midsentence as someone else came up to offer congratulations. I turned instead to Shirley, not sure what I was going to say but needing to say something. Shirley too turned away as another guest approached to speak to her. I was left floundering. I looked around wildly, not sure who to turn to. I didn't recognize any of the faces. I guessed that many of the people present were from Massacre or Roseau where Patsy probably worked. I was from Salisbury; most of my acquaintances came from there. I searched frantically for a way out. Maybe I could turn and run away. Pretend I had never been there.

Instead, I stood rooted to the spot, shocked beyond belief. As far as I knew, Ian was already married. He had told me himself. Maybe if I hadn't stepped out of the ceremony, I might have been able to do something. Surely, it was too late now? Maybe I could tell Shirley, or the bride herself. But would anyone believe me? I spotted the priest at the buffet table and felt a surge of hope. Yes, I could tell a priest. He'd know what to do. I started slowly towards him, keeping my eyes fixed on him, in case he moved. I was almost at his side when someone spoke to me.

"Hello, Mercury. Nice to see you again."

Pleasantly said, but with a decided chill. It could only have been one person. I recognized his voice even before I turned to him. It was Ian, of course. Smilingly, he extended his hand in my direction. He was dressed like most of the men present: black trousers, white shirt, black bow tie, and red sash. Only, unlike the others, he wore a jacket with a white rose pinned on. He was sweating slightly; not in trickles, but a film of sweat over his whole face. He smiled with his mouth, but his eyes were watchful. Not cold, but not warm either. As if it all depended on me.

"Hi, Ian. Are you the groom?"

He nodded but remained silent.

"Right." I paused for a moment, trying to find the right words. I couldn't find any, so I just said the first thing that came to mind. "Ian, I thought you said you were married?"

"Did I? You must be mistaken. I've never been married."

"Ian, don't you remember our conversation at the hotel? You said that your wife had gone to visit her relatives in Australia."

"Mercury, you're mistaken. I said I've never been married. But I think you had better leave."

"Leave? But I came with Shirley. I've got to go back with her."

Now, his eyes were cold. Frosty. Warning me not to interfere. He wanted me to leave his wedding. I hardly knew Shirley, and I definitely didn't know Patsy. She looked happy to be married to her Ian. They had a child together. Maybe she already knew and consented to marry him anyway. Who was I to care? I was no one's saviour. I looked up at Ian and nodded. "Okay, I'll leave. But this may not be the end."

"It had better be, Mercury. I won't let you or anybody else upset my wife. I'll show you to the car park."

And so, I left without even saying good-bye to Shirley. I made my way home as best as I could and arrived confused and tired. As expected, Shirley came to find me at my mum's, but I was asleep and my mum wouldn't wake me. She wondered why I had left so early. Apparently, the groom had said that he had spoken to me and I had decided to leave because I had felt unwell. Nice.

I thought about going to Shirley's to explain on a number of occasions, but I ached all the time. I was always tired, always sleepy. Each time I thought of heading out the door, my resolve crumbled and I headed back to bed.

That is where I was when Marcia came calling. Only she wouldn't come in. My mum came knocking on my door. "Your friend want you. She say it important. Come on, *lass coushai. Ou toh feyan*" —stop lying there. You're too lazy.

I struggled up only to flop down again on the settee in the living room. Marcia was still blowing her horn. My mum took up position at the front door. I could see that she'd been ironing. She had a small coal pot next to the table, with a couple of flat irons warming up. Freshly ironed clothes were laid out over the backs of the dining chairs. I knew from experience that as soon as she finished, she would start her tirade: "Can you people come and put the clothes away? At my age, I shouldn't be doing any ironing. Come on, put away the coal pot and get those clothes out of my living room." It was always the same script. Since I never had any clothes among the lot, I usually ignored her and wandered back to bed. This time, though, I perked up at the thought of seeing Marcia. I hadn't seen her since my arrival all those months ago. It seemed liked forever. Marcia was impatient:

"Mercury, come on, girl; let's go and bathe in the river."

I laughed and got up instantly. A river bath. I couldn't resist that. That was one of the few things I hadn't yet found time to do. Maybe I could talk to Marcia about the wedding? See what she thought? Marcia's wisdom was far beyond her years and definitely far beyond mine. I grabbed a few things and left with my mum looking on disapprovingly. I don't think she liked Marcia very much. She didn't approve of Marcia's dreadlocks or her cohabiting. But deep down, I think she was resentful that we were so close or that Marcia had such a great influence on me. But I didn't care anymore. I was an adult. I could have had worse friends than Marcia. Maybe my mum should be a bit more grateful that in spite of my apparent eccentricity, I invariably stayed on the straight and narrow.

I think life turned me into a loner. The burden of my guilt caused me to retreat into a shameful silence. Guilt at having been the object of abuse of a grown man. The shame of not having disclosed. Maybe my mum treated me so badly because she too felt guilty about what happened. Or maybe she was just ashamed of having a daughter who had been abused. She obviously held me in great contempt. It was a pity she didn't feel the need to love me more. Definitely, I needed to think about going back to England where I could be bold and strong and where I could hide in my tower of anonymity.

As I entered Marcia's vehicle, I felt an instant sense of peace. With Marcia, there was no need to hide. She understood without words. She was the soul mate I had never found in a man. Distance hadn't managed to cool our friendship. We'd hardly communicated over the last twenty years, but we both knew without doubt that we were still firm friends. Marcia was intelligent and talented and should have gone on to great things, but poverty had robbed her of a bright future. She had ended up conforming to the stereotype of her circumstances. We both had attended the same secondary school in Roseau—the Blessed Order School for Girls. She was very capable but had missed a lot of school due to severe bronchitis. Even when she was well, she was absent a lot, taking care of her ailing aunt. Both of Marcia's parents were still alive, but for some reason, she had been brought up by her aunt. She never visited her parents, and her mum only came to see her at school. She never saw her dad. Marcia never explained why even when I'd asked. But the school must have known because the teachers were happy for Marcia to leave her class and walk with her mum in the nearby Botanic Gardens. It had been and still was a great mystery.

Anyway, Marcia went straight to work after high school. The rest of us carried on to college, and later, most of us moved abroad. Marcia fell in love with the owner of the store where she worked. Jason, his name was. He was at least fifteen years older than Marcia and controlled her every move—what she wore, who she saw, how she spoke, where she went. But it was all done in the name of love, and Marcia didn't seem to mind. In my humble opinion, Jason was a creep. Short and stocky, he spent most of his time grooming himself. He would take his comb out of his pocket and run it through his wavy hair while serving customers or talking or even walking. I would enter their store, and he would say, "Ah Mercury, looking good; long time no see. Who's stirring your coffee these days?" Then the comb would come out of his back pocket and he would leer unpleasantly as he coiffed himself.

Jason, to say the least, was not a pleasant-looking man. He had bulging, bloodshot eyes, and his teeth resembled a dog's. Four short incisors and two long, pointed canines. His nose was flabby and squashed as if broken in a fight. His hands were always sweaty. But for some reason—maybe a few hidden assets!—he seemed to be quite popular with the ladies. I have no idea what a lovely girl like Marcia saw in him, but she appeared to revel in his love: "Jason cooked me dinner last night"; "Jason wants me to have his children"; "Jason said I'm the best girlfriend he ever had." I listened patiently, but, whenever I met him, I found it hard to reconcile the man to the stories. He just looked creepy.

Actually, as I recall, Marcia had had a boyfriend when she first met Jason, and Jason had been seeing one of the girls who worked for him. I found out much later that the four of them went out for a drink one evening and realized that they were attracted to each other's partner. I don't know if they actually discussed switching or if they just slowly drifted into relationships with each other's partner, but Marcia's boyfriend married the other girl, and Marcia ended up living with Jason. I would have loved to find out the details, but Marcia was tight-lipped. Not like me, always talking about my affairs.

When I entered her car, Marcia was upset, but I didn't realize it at first. I talked excitedly about seeing her again and asked about the girls. I wanted to know what was her experience of the hurricane, and only noticed her watery eyes and quavering mouth when she failed to answer.

"Marcia," I said sharply, "what's wrong? What's the matter?"

I was very concerned. Marcia was always fine, always bubbly. I was the one with all the baggage while she had all the answers.

"I'll tell you later," she mumbled.

"Is it something to do with the girls?" I asked.

"No," she answered, shortly. We carried on for a while in silence, and then she turned to me. "How far gone are you?"

"How far gone? I don't understand. Far gone how?" I was confused.

"Well, you're pregnant, aren't you?"

"*I'm what?*"

She took her eyes off the road for a frightening couple of seconds and looked at me strangely, as if to say, "Why are you denying it?"

"Well, you're pregnant, aren't you?" She repeated. Marcia must have seen my genuine look of horror, for she suddenly looked contrite and covered her mouth. "Oh no, Mercury, you mean you didn't know?"

"Know? Know what? Marcia, I don't understand. How do you mean, 'am I pregnant?'"

"Well, Mercury, you just look pregnant to me. I mean, I was looking at you coming down the steps of your mum's house; I just saw a pregnant woman. That's all."

I was stunned! Pregnant? Pregnant!

"Oh God, Marcia, I really look pregnant to you? I didn't know…" My voice trailed off into nothing. I fell silent. I was stricken. A small, dull ache started deep in my heart and filled my whole being.

I believed Marcia. She was right. I must be pregnant. I believed it without a shadow of a doubt. That was the cause of my moodiness, weight gain, and lethargy. I was carrying Lennox's child. I shivered and cupped my face in my hands. *Agnes, Agnes.* At my age, though, I should have known. But I had never been pregnant before. Gosh, my mum. She must have had the same suspicion. No wonder she thought I was a hypocrite. And now Marcia. I couldn't believe I had fallen pregnant to a man I didn't respect and never wanted to see again.

I shook my head to clear my thoughts and found that Marcia had pulled onto the side of the road. She laid a tentative hand on my shoulder and frowned in concern. I glanced at her and then turned to look out of the window at the barrenness all around. Empty, that's how I felt then, just empty. I wasn't sure if Marcia knew Lennox. I had told her my story but not who had done it. Lennox was very popular, and she probably did know him; at least by sight. I wasn't planning to tell her about him now. I breathed in deeply. "Marcia, yes, I think you might be right," I whispered.

"But you sounded like you didn't know."

Her voice was plaintive. Maybe she sensed my unhappiness. "I just wasn't expecting it," I replied. I looked at her then. She too looked quite full in her floral top. Her face was much broader than I remembered. I remember thinking that day in town that she looked pregnant, so I took another hard look at her.

"Marcia, but you look pregnant as well."

She nodded slowly. "I am." Then her face clouded over and I noticed afresh the tight lines around her mouth and her bloodshot eyes.

"Marcia, you seemed upset when I got in. What's the matter, then?"

Her face fell again. She studied me for a moment, as if pondering whether to confide in me. I wasn't sure that she would. Marcia was a very private person. But if she had a real problem, there were few people on the island she could talk to. I was a safe bet. I was only passing through, after all.

"It's Jason," she said quietly. "He got married in Tortola."

"Jason?" I spluttered. "But, but I thought you guys were still together?"

"We were." Her voice went even more quiet. "He went to buy stuff for the store and got stranded there when the hurricane struck."

"Marcia, I am so sorry. But why? Why did he do it?" I asked, perplexed.

She sniffed, but looked up. I sensed that she was growing stronger as she spoke. "He said that he wasn't coming back to see *mizeh*"—misery—"in Dominica. Some woman offered to marry him so he went ahead."

"But what about you and the girls?" I really was flabbergasted. I just couldn't make any sense of it.

Marcia took a deep breath. "He said that after he process his papers, he will send for us."

Right. Twisted male logic, as usual. Break the heart of your partner and children by marrying someone else for papers, then divorce your new partner and send for your old family to join you in your new country. I think that's why I disliked men so much. They just never seemed to be able to do anything right. Always thinking about themselves.

I comforted Marcia the best I could, but there wasn't much I could do to make things better. She just had to travel the cold, lonely road of heartbreak and rejection by herself.

"Did you tell him about the new baby?" I asked.

She shook her head dumbly, just looking tortured.

"No?" I enquired incredulously. "You didn't tell him?"

"Mercury, my life is such a mess. I'm in so much trouble." Marcia was weeping openly now. "Oh God, please forgive me."

I really was concerned about Marcia. I had never seen her this upset or known her to be anything but strong and righteous. I put a comforting arm around her.

"Mercury, the baby..." She stopped.

"The baby? Is something wrong with the baby?"

"It's not—" she took a longish pause—"it's not Jason's." The last bit was said in a rush, as if she were anxious to get the words out, finally.

I was utterly and completely stunned. Not Jason's baby? I mean, I would understand if I had been talking to someone else; not Marcia. Marcia was the most level-headed girl I knew. Plus, she was a Christian, actively involved in her church and prayer meetings.

"Well, whose is it then, if not Jason's?" I don't think my question was really addressed to Marcia. I was more or less thinking aloud. I would never ask Marcia anything that personal. But she answered anyway.

"It's for my pastor."

"Your pastor?" I was confused.

"Yeah you don't know him." She mumbled quickly. "It's a small church, Christ Temple."

My heart literally stopped beating. But I had to ask. "Christ's Temple? I thought that was in Salisbury. But you live in Coulibistri."

She looked at me sharply, suspicious, no doubt, of my knowledge. She bit her lip. "There's a branch in Coulibistri."

"You mean, you pregnant for Lennox?" I was shouting in spite of myself, reverting instinctively to my Dominican vernacular.

Marcia had a strange look on her face. "Lennox?" Her voice was a whisper. "You know Lennox?"

"Of course I bloody know him, Marcia. If I'm really pregnant, then I'm carrying his blasted child!"

I think it fair to say, that my words cut through Marcia as deeply as a knife. Her light literally went out at that moment. Nothing that she had been through up to that time had hurt her as profoundly. Her sense of betrayal was absolute. I had wielded the weapon that killed my friend's spirit. I tried to make sense of it, a lot later—Marcia had thought that she was special to Lennox. That afternoon, she learnt that she had been just another number. Worst of all, she realized that I wasn't in love with him, which made me stronger than she was. Always having been the top dog in our friendship, she resented that. But the complicity of our situation made her trust me more than she had previously.

One thing still puzzled me. "Marcia, how you so sure it's not Jason's child? I mean, you guys have been living together all this while. It might not be Lennox's, you know."

I think Marcia wished that I hadn't asked, but to her credit, she gave me an honest answer. Apparently, in the last two years of their relationship, Jason hadn't been the man that he had been previously—certain parts of his anatomy failing to rise to the occasion. Instead of discussing his difficulties with Marcia, he had chosen to attack, saying that it was her fault, that she had put on weight, that she put him under pressure, that she was too busy looking after the children. Suffice it to say, Marcia became increasingly frustrated and started noticing how attentive Pastor was to his American wife. Why couldn't Jason call her darling and hold hands with her in church? About the same time, Jason became very moody and stopped going to church. Susan, Lennox's wife, also started missing services with her difficult pregnancy, and Marcia took on a more hands-on role. Working late with Pastor and attending to his more personal needs meant a deepening intimacy, which culminated in a passionate yet brief encounter. But, after drinking of the forbidden cup a few times, Lennox decided it wasn't worth the risk. He was committed to his marriage. Marcia was crushed. She had fallen in love with him and wore her pain on her sleeve. Before long, Lennox forbade her to continue attending his church.

"'God spoke to me last night,' he said. 'Touch no unclean thing and I will receive you,' he said to me. 'Please, do not come back to this church.'"

Every painful word was delivered through racking sobs. I too cried silently as I listened to Marcia reliving her ordeal. I remembered Susan and her wounds of love. Even her devotion hadn't saved her from the wrath of the beast. For the first time, I thought how lucky I'd been to escape with my dignity intact.

Only, now, I had spawned a monster. I, too, was carrying Lennox's child. Then I had an idea.

"Marcia"—I was suddenly hesitant—"don't you think that now Susan is, um, gone, Lennox might change his mind?"

I wasn't prepared for the wail that followed.

"I already asked him. I asked him! He turned me down! He said the child wasn't his, and I should get off his property."

Marcia was suddenly calm. As if she were listening to the words sink afresh into her throbbing heart. She took a deep breath and wiped her eyes. Slowly, her wild gaze refocused. I looked out and saw that night had fallen without us noticing.

We had pulled up at the Tarish pit, a sort of quarry, just opposite the Layou River. In the dark, it was just an oily shimmer. I thought about how easy it would be to start driving and keep going into its glistening depths. But Marcia spoke and said we had to head back. She had left Rhya and Evageline with her aunt. I wished I could have offered her some hope, a way out of her situation. Lennox liked and respected me. He had asked me to marry him. Surely he would listen to me? I didn't say anything to Marcia, but I had made a decision: I would speak to Lennox on her behalf. Maybe, just maybe, I could work a miracle.

Chapter 10

I had decided to return to England. It wasn't a difficult decision. I was pregnant and showing. Dominica was moribund, breathing the gasping breath of a dying giant. I could see no future here for myself or my child. Plus, I was in a terrible quandary about telling Lennox about our child; I didn't want him complicating things, like insisting that I stay in Dominica. It would be much easier to tell him from England, I decided. So, I set a date for my departure. But, before then, one clear Saturday morning, I set out to find Lennox.

Mero wasn't far from Salisbury, about forty minutes at a leisurely pace, I think. My mum's house was on a hill overlooking the playing field and sea, right at the entrance to *Cuba Road*. Everything was dry around that time. But the flamboyant trees which had remained standing were now in bloom. Their deep red flowers opened irreverently to reveal long, sticky yellow stamens which hung limply out of their virginal funnels. The sea sparkled sleepily at the far end of the village. I could smell it even at that distance. It smelled of fresh fish and salt. Not all seas smelled like that. In Europe, the sea smelled as if it hadn't been salted enough. I breathed in deeply as I set off. This was the smell of home. But I still didn't feel like I belonged. I felt like I had sold my birthright for a lie. I was more at home in Europe than in my native land.

There were some sharp corners on the right hand side of the road, so I walked on the left. The sea receded behind wide cliffs and soon, I lost sight of it. I was left with my thoughts. I didn't know what I was going to say to Lennox. I wished I could love him. That would make everything right. I could marry him, and we would raise our child together. As it was, I was going to try to sell him the idea of another woman as his bride. I worried about Marcia's two children. Lennox had raped minors before, although I'm sure he didn't see it as rape. Rape was an ugly word that men preferred not to use. Maybe he thought he was entitled to what was on offer. Or he genuinely didn't think of the effect his actions would have on such young lives. Then, again, maybe he thought women were inherently inferior to men. Always available for his pleasure. Maybe I just hated the bastard. Maybe I wished I could reverse the clock and never be born. Maybe I just needed God.

The road was virtually deserted, but I wasn't scared. There was nothing to be scared off. Dominica was in mourning. An old man and woman with a donkey went past, heading in the opposite direction. They didn't make eye contact, but I said "morning" anyway. I didn't get an answer. The woman walked slightly ahead, carrying a small cooking pot tied in a cloth. The man was stooped and sullen, but led the donkey gently enough by the bridle. It was laden to the brim with what looked like household goods. I wondered if they were moving from Salisbury to Mero. Or maybe St. Joseph? More likely to be St. Joseph. I felt a bit guilty then. Since coming to Dominica, I had become so engrossed in my problems that I hadn't found time to help anyone. It had been all about me. These people were suffering with no real hope for their future, but I was still relatively well off. In one reckless move, I had sold my flat in London to fund my excursion of revenge. I hadn't cared that I would be homeless on my return. I had just wanted Lennox to pay for his sins. Now, I was pregnant by the devil. Would that make my child demon or angel? I was scared. I needed a saviour.

I had just gone past Macoucherie and was ambling down the final hill before the Bay in Salisbury when a pick- up truck drove past me at top speed, in the opposite direction. To be honest, I was deep in thought and only caught a glimpse of it. But it screeched to a halt, and I could hear the gears put noisily into reverse. I looked up as it stopped next to me.

"Agnes!"

I shivered at the sound of my name. I had heard it said in exactly those tones, so many times in the last months. My heart leapt within me. It was Lennox, of course. I felt a strange joy, and a longing to be in his company. I didn't understand that. I always thought I hated him. Maybe I was more depressed than I realized. I shook my head to clear my thoughts.

Lennox was going for a river bath, he said. Did I want to go along? I agreed, of course. I hadn't had the chance to go to the river in all this time. Marcia and I had never made it that day. We had been overcome by the intensity of our stories. Plus, it would be easier to talk to Lennox out in the open. I got into his vehicle happily enough. He didn't say anything, just smiled and set off. I, too, hardly said a word. I didn't need to. I felt at peace, like I belonged next to him.

Macoucherie was an old colonial estate which had fallen into disrepair. Mostly coconuts and sugar cane grew there, with a few mango trees. It looked quite small from the main road. All that could be seen was the cone-shaped exit of the river on one side of the short bridge which spanned its banks before it disappeared behind some mangrove bushes on the opposite side. I knew that it culminated in a small sandy beach where it met the sea, although this wasn't visible from the road. The long, meandering entrails of the river as it left its mountain source remained a mystery because it couldn't be seen unless one drove up the private road within the estate itself.

Macoucherie was a big part of my childhood and an important adjunct to Salisbury in those days. Apart from employing some of the villagers as labourers, it served as a receiving station for bananas, at the height of the industry. A boxing plant was built close to the main road, and there, the fruit was weighed, washed, packed, and readied for shipping. It was then taken to the bay at Salisbury and out to the waiting ship by schooner. I also remembered the sweet smell of pressed cane and distilling rum, as well as the heady smell of *copra*, coconuts dried in a kiln. Much of the time, the ladies of the village headed to the river to do their laundry, as the small stream near the church in Salisbury only flowed after very heavy rainfall. The Macoucherie River was always steady and strong. I had gone there often with the woman who worked as our maid. The river was still full, seemingly untouched by the hurricane.

In no time, Lennox turned into the rocky road leading into the estate. Like everywhere else, it had been stripped of its beauty and lay in an untidy mess. The roof had been lifted off the boxing plant, but the concrete troughs previously used for washing bananas remained intact. They stood in rows like empty bassinets in a hospital nursery. To the right, a few breadfruit trees remained. I could see hordes of flies buzzing around the rotting fruit underneath. Straight ahead, on a small hill, stood the old plantation house, constructed entirely of stone. A stony track led to some rusty gates, which shut the house away from the public. It looked perfect from my vantage point, but I couldn't say if it had suffered any damage from the hurricane.

It was a bumpy and uncomfortable ride. I was more than four months pregnant, now. My complexion was changing slowly. My face was streaked a darker black in places, and my nostrils flared slightly. But I was blooming all over. I looked relaxed and happy. I had stopped worrying about the future and had decided to enjoy my pregnancy. I had waited long enough for the privilege, as it was. I still hadn't told Lennox about it. Nor did I intend to, now. Instead, I planned to try to persuade him to marry Marcia. If he agreed, I would then tell her about his actions. It would be her decision then.

"Ouch!" I cried out instinctively as Lennox rode over a large flat boulder lying in the road. I hadn't paid much attention to his driving before, but he was flying over the bumpy track, steering to the right and left with abandon as he negotiated the stones and potholes which served as a road.

"You okay? Sorry, man. This road is a challenge."

"I can see that," I said rather sharply. "Be careful; we ladies are fragile, you know."

"Okay, don't panic, I'll slow down."

The silence broken, I decided to address a few of the things which were on my mind. But, I knew I had to tread carefully. I didn't want Lennox losing his temper and aborting our outing. I really wanted to spend some time at the river and, also, I needed time to persuade him to consider Marcia as a life partner. I looked at him as tenderly as I could.

"Don't you get lonely, Lennox, now that Susan's gone?"

He nodded briefly but kept his eyes on the road.

"Well, why don't you marry again?"

He turned sharply and said harshly, "I asked you to marry me, Agnes, don't you remember? But you ran off!"

That was true. I had forgotten about the proposal or I might have phrased my question differently. I had been appalled by his offer. Then, marrying a snake had seemed a more enticing prospect. I still didn't want him. I wondered again if I were doing the right thing in trying to connect him with Marcia. Real fears for the welfare of her children. But, I couldn't forget the lost look on her face; her pain was obvious to see. My friend Marcia was in love with her Pastor. I owed it to her to help.

I paused to review my strategy. I needed to try to reach a part of Lennox that I had never reached before. I sensed that I needed to be gentle. Understanding. Maybe, even loving. So, I tried again.

"Lennox, I'm sorry. It was so unexpected that I panicked. Thank you for asking me." Perhaps a tiny lie was also in order: "But you know, I have someone back in the UK; I'm not really free."

"Lucky guy."

"Well, Lennox, you too were lucky to have Susan. And now you have Marcia," I added without thinking.

"Marcia? You know Marcia?"

Well, there was no running away now. "Yes, she and I went to school together."

He opened his mouth to speak but I cut in quickly. "Lennox, she loves you, why don't you give her a chance?"

Lennox took his eyes off the road for a moment, searching my face as if to decipher my trustworthiness. "You want to know why, Agnes? I'll tell you why. I can't trust Marcia. If she can betray her man, what will she do to me?"

"She loves you. Plus, things were not too great between her and Jason."

"Yeah, you women always say that. But Marcia is not my type. I'm looking for a solid woman."

"A solid woman?" That was unexpected. "Lennox, Marcia is beautiful and very talented. I don't understand why you don't see her that way."

"Marcia has nothing to offer me, Agnes. I'm looking for a woman with a degree or something. A woman who can make me proud. I'm not going to marry a bloody seamstress!"

Right. Mr. Bigshot. What could I say to him now? I decided to point out the obvious. "Lennox, but as far as

I know, you don't have a degree, either. Isn't that asking too much of her?"

He lifted his stubbled chin proudly. "I am a pastor. I am filled with the spirit of God. He will only give me the best."

I was angry now. "Lennox, how can you be filled with the spirit of God when you've hurt so many people? Look at how you treated your wife… and me," I added for good measure.

"Agnes, you need to read your bible. All have sinned and fall short of the glory of God. Christ died for my sins."

"Yes, but doesn't repentance mean change? Aren't you supposed to ask for forgiveness of the people you've hurt and turn over a new leaf?"

"I haven't hurt anybody. My life is hidden with Christ in God. Henceforth, let no man trouble me."

I was frustrated. Lennox was quoting the bible to me, but it made no sense. He didn't seem to think it necessary to live a godly life. To him, being a pastor of some obscure church that he started himself was an end in itself. "Lennox, what do I need to do to be saved?"

My gosh, where on earth did that come from? I didn't want to be saved. I just wanted to be at peace. I didn't want to be a Christian if Lennox was one. But somehow, I had just asked Lennox about being saved.

His answer was swift. "Believe in the Lord Jesus Christ."

"I believe. I believe in Jesus. But then, what? Lots of people believe in Jesus. Even thieves and murderers. That doesn't make them saved."

He remained silent. Perhaps he sensed a trap. But I wasn't trying to trap him. I just couldn't see. I would genuinely embrace Christianity if it made sense. This man believed, but he was evil. Why would I follow an evil person?

"All I know, Agnes, is that God forgave my sins. I am now free."

He turned away, his face saying not to ask him any more questions. I fell silent. Lennox drove more slowly, looking for somewhere to stop. I had been so intent on talking, that I hadn't noticed the surroundings. We had already travelled a fair distance up the road into Macoucherie. I had never been that far before because it would have been too far to walk. It seemed like the whole estate was tightly squeezed into a narrow valley. To the right was the flowing river, ridden with fallen stones and boulders. The water eased its way gingerly around each obstacle, meeting again triumphantly on the other side. Sometimes it would deepen into a large pool called a *bassin*, which is pronounced like the French, where people could enjoy bathing. The river itself was dominated by a large cliff of solid rock and wild vines. The only arable land was to the left, bounded again by a smaller cliff. Sometimes the land narrowed into a small strip; at other times, it widened into a larger field. But always, it was dotted with rocks and boulders. However, there didn't seem to be much devastation from the hurricane. Most of the cacao and mango trees were still standing, although there were a few fallen coconut trees. They seemed fragile and sad.

Lennox had stopped and was putting the truck in reverse, ready to back into a spot next to the river. A grass verge led to a rocky path, just wide enough for a vehicle. I couldn't see beyond that because of the length of the cab.

"Here we are then, Miss U.K."

Lennox was smiling again, showing his sparkling white teeth. He looked so engaging when he smiled. I could forgive him anything then. He removed his cap and placed it casually in my lap, as if handing me a part of himself. At the same time, he slid his other arm along the back of my seat and leant into me, breathing heavily. I was sure he was going to kiss me, but he suddenly reached for the clasp of the glove compartment and grabbed some soap. Then he tapped me playfully on the knee.

"You coming for a bath?"

"I would love to, but I don't have a swimsuit."

"You can bathe in your clothes," he proffered. "It's so hot that they'll dry again before we leave."

"Actually," I said excitedly, "that's a great idea!"

I got out of the truck and headed for the water's edge. It was so peaceful, yet foreboding. Maybe because there was no one else around. Or, because of the dark shadows gathering here and there, where the light fell short. Or maybe just the sound of the river, constant and relentless, moaning and complaining as it made its long, bumpy journey down to the sea. I shivered slightly and wrapped my arms around myself. I headed for a spot of sunlight just a little way up from where I was standing. I glanced back and saw Lennox washing the truck with a sponge and bucket.

I made my way gingerly along the slippery rocks, spreading my arms wide to balance at times. Not that it was dangerous. The water was quite shallow. I just didn't want to get my feet wet. I reached my vantage point and sat down heavily. I was strangely tired, burdened. I tried to understand why. Everything was OK, so why wasn't I happy inside? I was tired of being alone, I think. Tired of running away. I was going to have a baby and I wanted to offer it a normal home—with a mummy and a daddy and, later, a brother or a sister. Should I let bygones be bygones and accept Lennox's offer? Could people change their character? Become better people? Would Lennox always be a cheat and a wife beater? Or could I inspire and change him. Could he be good for me in any way?

I mused with my eyes shut, and I think I fell asleep. I saw myself alone in the middle of an expanse of arid land. Everything was completely barren, with a solitary leafless tree over on the horizon. The ground was completely parched and cracked, not sandy like in a desert but broken like a dried lake. I was naked except for a wispy cloth around my pregnant body. I was in labour and searching for somewhere to have my baby. I don't know why I was alone. There was no one else in sight. I didn't seem to belong to any community. As I watched, the earth seemed to move and pucker up along the edges, moving towards me like a small wave. I couldn't make any sense of it. The wave grew bigger and more agitated, wriggly-like. It was almost upon me when I realized that it wasn't a wave after all but a heaving, scary mass of snakes. I screamed silently, turning to run, but they were behind me, bearing down. As I watched, petrified, the cracks closer to me started breaking and tiny, twisting snakes began oozing out of them.

By then, I was in agony, writhing in pain. My baby was ready to be born, and I needed to lie down. I searched frantically for a safe spot, but there were snakes everywhere, gliding and entwining in a terrifying dance. As I searched, there was a massive rumble and everything stopped. The wave itself stood up and hung there in midair, as if frozen. The ground opened right in front of me, and a huge snake like an alligator rose from the ground. It uncoiled slowly, like a king rising from his throne, shaking its head groggily. As it straightened, it looked at me. Its eyes were as huge and round as tennis balls, stained a dark red colour. Straw-like whiskers hung from the sides of its mouth. It looked at me intently for a few seconds and then appeared to break into a smile. Two barbaric fangs unfolded from its upper jaw, and then it roared. By then, my baby was forcing its way out, and I sank to the ground. I strained back, not touching the ground, just stretching back, with a hand out in support. With my other hand, I reached for my baby's head as it poked out. I screamed as the baby burst forth in a final effort, and as it did, the snake shook itself with a roar and lunged. I was screaming and fighting for air as I awoke to Lennox's touch. He was shaking me and calling my name, "Agnes, Agnes! Come on; you're dreaming. Wake up."

I awoke gasping and trembling, scared out of my wits by what I had experienced. "Lennox, oh my God, Lennox!" I held on to him like child, seeking comfort.

"What was it? What were you dreaming about?"

"My baby," I gasped. "A snake was waiting to eat my baby."

A strange look came over his face. "Your baby?" he echoed. "You're having a baby?"

I looked up dumbly, realizing what I had just said.

"Is it my child, Agnes?" He asked, reaching for my top and pulling it away to expose my bulging stomach.

I lay defenceless, my belly exposed for Lennox to see. A faint black line ran from my navel all the way down to my pubic area. Before I could stop him, Lennox reached out his large hand and cupped the dome, his head coming down and resting on my chest. I don't know which scared me most. The nightmare I just had or Lennox 's head perched loving on me. "Jesus," I whispered. Even in my head, it sounded like a whimper. I had seen Lennox's eyes as he looked at my bulge; they bore a wild, unearthly look.

"Susan," he said. "You've come back. You've given me my baby back."

I breathed in sharply. Susan, he thought I was Susan? Dared I explain who I was? Would he listen?

"Lennox," I said tenderly, "it's Agnes."

"Agnes?" He looked up quickly, looking but not seeing me. "Who's Agnes? Are you trying to trick me again, Susan? Why did you leave me, Susan? Why did you take my child away?" His face clouded over and he scowled suddenly. He got off me without warning, jerking me to my feet as he did so. He reached for my shoulders, pressing hard into my flesh. "I want my child, Susan; you're not going to take it away from me this time. I'm going to chain you up like a dog until you give birth!"

My heart grew deathly cold. Lennox's voice was chilling. I sensed that he was absolutely serious. I wondered if he had lost his senses. Maybe I could distract him and run away. But we were so far inland that he would overtake me with his truck. There was hardly any cover to hide. Lennox was pulling me roughly along the rocks, not caring that I slipped and slid like a rag doll.

"Lennox, it's Agnes, not Susan," I called out.

"I won't let you trick me again, Susan," he answered roughly. "I'm going to chain you like the dog you are."

I prayed silently. *Jesus, if you're alive, then help me.*

Lennox stopped suddenly and looked at me penetratingly as if trying to discern my features. "You're not Susan," he said confused. He looked again searchingly, still gripping my arm tightly. "You're Agnes!" he shouted suddenly. "You're Agnes, and you're having my baby."

I feared that I had escaped one calamity only to land in another.

Chapter 11

I left Dominica as quietly as I had come. I told no one, not even my family. I escaped with what was left of my dignity and sanity. I left by night on a boat leaving from the northern town of Portsmouth. I braved the rough voyage to Guadeloupe where I finally caught a plane to England. I had lost my baby in the fight with Lennox that day. He had left me for dead by the river and sped off. As the light around me closed in, finally veering off into nothingness, I prayed silently to God to save my life. Or, at least, to receive me into his kingdom. I asked for forgiveness for my sins. I confessed Jesus as Lord and Saviour. I had heard the formula enough times to know what was required of me in my final hour. I wasn't going to let pride stop me from enjoying a peaceful afterlife. If hell and eternal damnation awaited the nonbelieving, then I wanted no part of it.

God must have had pity on me for he saved me. I woke up in the arms of a Rastafarian couple who lived in isolation in the heights of the Macoucherie estate. When I first regained consciousness, I thought myself in the throes of hell. Flames were licking lustily at my body and I could hear myself screaming even before I awoke. But my hell was only the pangs of childbirth. I writhed and shrieked as my premature son emerged from my warm body. I saw his small, still form covered in sticky white paste and turned away as Martha received him into one of her blankets.

"Would you like to hold him?" she asked, approaching.

I shook my head quickly. "Just bury him, please, Martha," I whispered. I couldn't bear the pain of holding him. I knew that I would never give him back. As she disappeared with my son, my joy ebbed slowly from my soul, and I descended into a bleak depression.

I don't know how long exactly I stayed with Martha and Ras. It seemed like a lifetime. All I remember is lying still. After my baby was born, Ras lifted me off their bed and unto a pile of bedding in the corner of their sitting room. I lay there and stared at the ceiling for what seemed like months. Martha had to wash, feed, and clean my body of the evacuations, which poured out where I lay. Try as I might, I couldn't move a muscle. I was waiting to die. I thought I would close my eyes and wake next to my son in a dark, quiet garden.

One day, unexpectedly, my gloom lifted. I woke up, stretched, looked at Martha, and smiled.

"Ras," she shouted. "She's back; she's back!"

I laughed and held her in a grateful embrace. I knew beyond doubt that she had saved my life. Later, when I was strong and refreshed, they filled me in on the missing details of my story:

They had found me lying a pool of blood, right next to the path where we had parked by the river. At first, they had thought I was dead, but Martha had heard a faint groan, and Ras lifted me and slung me over his shoulder. They carried me to their little house up in the hills of Macoucherie. God knows what a dead weight I must have been. Ras was tall and as slim as a reed. His *ital* diet con-

tained very little fat, and he worked hard growing food for the market in St. Joseph. In the evenings, he would light up a fat s*plif* and read aloud from his bible. Martha and I would gather round and listen to his rhythmic tones:
"O Lard, my strengt' an fartress
My refuge in time of distress
To you the nation-them will come
From di ends of di ert' and say
Our father-them possess nortin' but false gads."

"Agnes, man you've been fallowin false gads. Jah is di one true gad. He is di Alpha and di Omega; di beginnin' and di end."

I nodded. It all made sense, finally. I didn't need anyone to explain it anymore. Only Jesus could save me. I looked at Ras. "Yes, I understand. From now and forever, I will follow him."

"What about dis man who attack you. What you go do 'bout him?"

"I forgive him. I will go back to England now." I hadn't thought about those words, but as I said them, I understood that this was what I had to do.

The next day, I sent Ras and Martha to my mum's house with a list of things I needed for my journey. I only wanted a few clothes and my handbag. I was planning to make a fresh start. I would carry Dominica in my heart, but I wanted nothing to remind me of the awful experiences I'd had.

A few days later, Ras borrowed his uncle's van, and he and Martha drove me to Portsmouth, where it was easy to get a boat leaving for Guadeloupe. I hugged them tightly, ever grateful for the love they had shown me, a stranger.

"God bless you forever," I whispered. I had left them an envelope with a large present under their pillow at home. Martha would find it when changing their bedclothes. By then, I would be far away in my adopted land.

It was dusk when the boat finally pulled away from the shore. There was still no electricity on the island. Lights popped up intermittently like watchful, glowing eyes around the town. Sometimes, the bright, clear lights from a generator flared, but mostly, it was the ghostly glow of kerosene lamps or candles. I found a lit corner on the deck and took out the small bible Ras had given to me. I opened at random and found this passage:

Beyond all question, the mystery of godliness is great:
He appeared in a body,
Was vindicated by the Spirit,
Was seen by angels,
Was preached among the nations,
Was believed on in the world,
Was taken up in glory.

I settled back and pondered on the "mystery of godliness." I liked the thought of a God. Not because of what he could do for me, but because I needed to worship. It was the ultimate emptying of myself. The ultimate path to my liberty. I offered up my spirit to my invisible God and felt my joy return. I could look forward to a rewarding future without the dark echoes of the past. I had found peace: I had tamed my hurricane.

The End

Biography

One of seven children, the author, Paula A. John comes from the Island of Dominica, in the West Indies. Village life in the late 60s - early 70s provided an endless supply of adventure and stories which serve as a backdrop for much of her book.

Paula has a degree in French and taught at one of the secondary schools in Dominica before emigrating to Britain in 1994, where she trained as a nurse. Now in her mid-forties, Paula has just completed an MA in Linguistics at the University of Manchester. She has two daughters who share her love for travel, fashion and creative writing. Together, they spent a year in Malta and, again, their experiences are reflected in the stories and characters of the novel. 'Taming A Hurricane' is Paula's first book and, in many ways, reflects her interest in 'language'. Paula is a Christian and believes that 'God' belongs to the people. This book reflects one person's attempt to touch him.

Printed in Great Britain
by Amazon